"You trust too much, Gemma." Grayson stepped closer.

"I think you're right," she replied. "I trust people I don't even know. Like you. I trust you when I shouldn't. I don't even know you."

How could he make her understand he was here to help her? But that wasn't true, either. What was he thinking? Helping Gemma Rollins had never been part of his mission parameters. He was here to finish this, to find the man who was not only responsible for Bill's death but who was also the head of a large wildlife trafficking ring.

"Listen, Gemma, I was looking for you to tell you about an idea I came up with."

Her eyes brightened. "You came up with an idea for me? What—"

A rumble above cut off her question. Rocks shifted overhead, crashed against the cliffside, and echoed across the mountain and through the trees.

"Look out!" Grayson grabbed Gemma, cane and all, and pressed her beneath a protruding part of the rock wall, covering her with his body. Protecting her. Her breaths came hard and fast against his neck as her fear mingled with his own.

God, please protect her. Protect us!

Elizabeth Goddard is an award-winning author of more than twenty novels, including the romantic mystery *The Camera Never Lies*–winner of a prestigious Carol Award in 2011. After acquiring her computer science degree, she worked at a software firm before eventually retiring to raise her four children and become a professional writer. In addition to writing, she homeschools her children and serves with her husband in ministry.

Books by Elizabeth Goddard

Love Inspired Suspense

Wilderness, Inc.

Targeted for Murder
Undercover Protector

Mountain Cove

Buried
Untraceable
Backfire
Submerged
Tailspin
Deception

Freezing Point
Treacherous Skies
Riptide
Wilderness Peril

Visit the Author Profile page at Harlequin.com.

UNDERCOVER PROTECTOR

ELIZABETH GODDARD

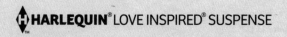

HARLEQUIN® LOVE INSPIRED® SUSPENSE

LOVE INSPIRED BOOKS

Recycling programs
for this product may
not exist in your area.

ISBN-13: 978-0-373-67798-6

Undercover Protector

www.Harlequin.com

Printed in U.S.A.

A righteous man has regard for the life of his animal,
But even the compassion of the wicked is cruel.
–Proverbs 12:10

For Mom

Acknowledgments

Thanks to my many dear writing friends
who have encouraged me along this journey.
I'm so blessed that God brought us together. I'm grateful
that God planted a dream in my heart and then made my
dream of telling stories come true. Special thanks to Jeri at
Crown Ridge Tiger Sanctuary for answering my questions
about these wonderful big cats and what it's like to
care for them in a sanctuary. I'm more than blessed to
have an editor who believes in my stories—thank you,
Elizabeth Mazer—and an agent who saw something in me
years ago—thank you, Steve Laube.

ONE

Siskiyou Mountains, southwest Oregon

Gemma Rollins shifted gears as her beloved Jeep CJ bounced over the narrow gravel road carved from the mountain. With this torrential downpour, she was glad she'd opted for the hard cover and doors on this older model.

But she should have gotten the mud tires too.

This was just like when the Pineapple Express came through southern Oregon a decade ago. Except spring was the wrong time of year for the tropical moisture to be sweeping in from the Hawaiian Islands. The meteorological phenomenon occurred in the winter.

And the tigers in her sanctuary, fifteen beautiful creatures she knew by name, wouldn't be happy in this inclement weather either.

Gemma downshifted, slowing at the curve on the steep one-lane road, her pulse edging up as the rain pounded harder. This was a lot more like the kind of weather she'd see in Houston, Texas, rather than southwest Oregon. And too much rain might cause flooding in the sanctuary. With a USDA inspection coming up in three weeks, she so did *not* need more hurdles in her goal of getting Tiger Mountain accredited as a big cat sanctuary.

She pressed her foot against the brakes as she came up on the switchback. Suddenly, the steering refused to turn. What was happening? The sharp bend approached. She would never make it!

Throwing her entire body into turning the steering wheel, Gemma's effort paid off. The CJ slid around the bend, though still much too close to the edge of the ravine.

Trees and rocks would slow anything trying to take a fall, but that didn't reassure her. Nearing the next curve, she pumped the brakes. They weren't working so well either.

She was behind in vehicle maintenance, no doubt there, but her CJ had never let her down before. Another curve in the road approached, and she shifted to the lowest gear, gripped the wheel with both hands and groaned with the effort to make the turn.

She'd driven the road that bordered the fenced-in area of the sanctuary enough times to know what to expect—more switchbacks. The road was dangerous on a good day. She hit the brakes harder. Still the CJ picked up more speed. She turned the steering wheel left, barely making another switchback.

Her beloved CJ was out of control.

Heart hammering, the realization slammed her—this was a matter of survival.

She might actually die. The possibility sucked her breath away.

Mud oozed from the rocky wall to her left as it poured from the hillside above. *God, please help me! I don't want to die today. And please keep the sanctuary intact. Please don't let those fences give way.*

She couldn't imagine that would happen, but, then again, she hadn't dreamed her steering would give way on the same day as her brakes. What were the chances? A question rose from the shadows in her mind. Had this been intentional?

And on a treacherous, rainy day.

Images from that night long ago accosted her. Headlights glinting off a wall of water. The grinding crunch. The wreck that left her uncle dead, the Tiger Hills sanctuary her father had founded dismantled and Gemma with nerve damage and a limp.

Focus, Gemma! She gripped the steering wheel tighter, mentally skimming the road ahead. Another bend. She'd never make it with her steering out like this. But if she could make it around the next outcropping of the rocky wall—before the dangerous bend—and remain on the road, there was an incline to her right, a turn out that she could use to slow the CJ to a stop.

Would it be enough?

Come on, come on, come on…

"God, if You're listening, and You don't want me to die today, I need some help." Gemma wrestled the wheel even harder and yanked the emergency brake, getting no return for her efforts.

Up ahead, mud and rocks washed over the road.

A mudslide!

Though it could be dangerous, deadly even, she could use the mudslide to slow the CJ, except she would have another battle for survival. But it was moving slowly enough she might just be able to make it.

Was that the answer to her prayer?

The incline appeared ahead in the thick of the mud. She pumped the brakes again, but they were completely dead. Gemma shifted into a higher gear and sped over the mud before it carried her away.

The roar of the torrential rain and the sight of the mudslide filled her with dread and morbid memories, erasing all other rational thought. Gemma fought the rising terror.

She gripped the wheel and steered toward the

incline, shifting down once she'd gained enough momentum because she'd need to stop this vehicle, once and for all, on the other side of the mud.

Regardless of her momentum, the CJ shifted as the mud gripped the tires, but Gemma persevered and evened out the pressure on the accelerator, adjusting her steering until the vehicle lifted up, the front tires gaining traction on the ground that rose above the mud, and sped forward.

But fast, much too fast.

The CJ slammed into a tree. Her body ricocheted against the seat belt. There were no airbags in an old Jeep CJ.

Stunned, Gemma blinked. Sucked in a breath. *I'm alive!*

Then she groaned.

"I'm alive." She breathed slowly to calm herself. "I'm…alive." It could have been much worse.

Gemma squeezed her eyes shut as memories overwhelmed her. Déjà vu. Her uncle had been driving the night he lost control of the vehicle and they hit a tree. He'd died and Gemma had lived. Why had she lived—then and now?

Drawing in a few more calming breaths until she could breathe normally, she shook away the daze. Felt the ache from her skin to her bones. But that was good news. She could feel everything, even the nerve damage pain in her left leg from the wreck that took Uncle Dave's life.

The CJ jerked to the right. What was going on?

Gemma turned her attention to the environment around her. The rain and the mud had risen even more and caught her rear tires. She had to hurry!

She tried to unbuckle her seat belt. Stuck. She searched for something sharp to cut herself out, but, strapped in the seat, she couldn't reach the tool kit in the back. Regardless, she tried to open the door, but it wouldn't budge. The front end had crumpled as the CJ twisted against the tree. Since she'd opted for a hard top, she couldn't cut her way out through the top, even if she could escape the seat belt trapping her inside.

She spied her cell phone—out of reach on the floorboard on the passenger side.

Gemma was going to die today, after all.

Grayson Wilde had picked the worst day for surveillance of the Tiger Mountain sanctuary. Now he paid the price as he searched for cover on the hillside to wait out the storm. He had an appointment in an hour to interview with Gemma Rollins, Tiger Mountain's founder, for a part-time volunteer position. A senior special agent for the United States Fish and Wildlife Service, Gray worked undercover to investigate and infiltrate a wildlife trafficking ring.

Shivering in the cold, he pushed deeper into

a shallow cave to shield himself from the brunt of the wind and rain while he waited it out. He scraped a hand over his face and wiped away the water. As miserable as it was to be in this place right at this moment, he reminded himself of the importance of his assignment. For starters, his mission in life was to thwart wildlife traffickers and poachers abusing God's creations. It was crucial, dangerous work, considering illegal exotic pet trade and trafficking had become a multibillion dollar industry, and came in right under drugs, firearms and human trafficking. And, as a source of funding for terrorist groups, it was a significant threat to both global and national security. But even aside from that, Gray had his own reasons for shadowing this sanctuary.

He'd gotten a tip from an informant that the person responsible for killing game warden Bill Garland—Gray's friend and mentor—was connected with the project. It was the kind of tip he'd been waiting on for what seemed like a lifetime. Bill had stumbled on a potential trafficking ring years ago, and turned the information over to the feds then ended up dead. With only two hundred fifty USFWS special agents to investigate the entire country, justice was never fully served.

And Gray needed a chance to make things right.

He had started as a game warden but worked

his way to becoming a federal agent and he finally had a solid lead on his ongoing investigation. Someone to connect with an extensive trafficking ring, though he didn't yet have a name.

His new mission was to gain Gemma Rollin's confidence and work the business with her so he could discover the truth. Find the person responsible for Bill's death. Arrest him and everyone else involved.

He might have to show up for the interview soaking wet, but that could work in his favor.

Over the deluge he thought he heard a cry for help. Who would possibly venture out in weather like this? Well, other than himself. But unless they were conducting surveillance and working undercover, nobody should be out in the wilderness region that hedged the tiger sanctuary.

Gray quieted his thoughts and listened.

There it was again, only this time it was not a cry for help but an actual scream.

He darted from the cave back into the rain, wishing for goggles—a snorkel and a pair of flippers might even work. "Where are you?"

But he wasn't sure how he could have heard the scream over the torrent to begin with and doubted they'd heard his response.

Careful of the slick ground, Gray made his way in the direction from which he thought the screams were coming. Then he found the road circling the tiger sanctuary.

That made sense. Someone could have been driving this and he wouldn't have seen it from his perch. He jogged down the twisted, muddy road, water pouring from the rocky wall to his left. The screams came louder but were muffled.

Gray ran around a curve in the road and saw the mud rushing down the mountain, eating away this portion of the road.

And he saw an old Jeep CJ shoved up into a tree. He searched for thin places in the rush of water and mud and did a dance with the forces of nature as he hopped, skipped, jumped and charged like a bull intent on his target. He caught the bumper, gripped it, holding on against the force of the liquid earth sliding under his feet. He made his way to the driver's side door.

A frantic woman sat inside, her mouth wide and halfway through the word *help* when she caught sight of him. She stopped and closed her mouth.

Assessing the situation, Gray didn't need her to explain the urgency or that she couldn't get her door open. He doubted climbing out the other side was even an option, since the vehicle hung precariously near the edge on the passenger side. He tried the door, using brute strength, and then kicked at it, but it wouldn't budge. If he'd brought his weapon, he might have been able to shoot the door mechanism so it would release.

Instead, he grabbed a large rock.

Her troubled eyes grew wide again.

"Unbuckle your seat belt!" he yelled over the roar. "And move out of the way."

"I can't!"

"I'm going to smash the window."

She nodded. Covering her face, she leaned away.

Gray hit the window. Glass shattered, falling everywhere inside the vehicle, including on the woman. She carefully tossed aside the bigger chunks, and Gray helped remove the rest. He pulled out his Buck knife from his jeans pocket, cut her seat belt and then tugged off his jacket, laying it over the window jamb to protect her. Gray planned to pull her out, but she climbed out herself, her agility surprising him until she fell to the ground. Her left leg appeared stiff, her expression one of agony.

"You're hurt!" He crouched next to her. Of course, she would be hurt after her Jeep had slammed into the tree.

Rain beating down on her, she tried to stand on her own but failed and slipped back, mere inches from the spreading river of mud.

"We have to get out of here before the mud carries us away along with your Jeep." Gray scooped her into his arms.

She struggled against him and reached for the vehicle. "No, wait! I need—"

"Unless you've got a child in there—" and Gray hadn't seen anyone else in the vehicle "—someone else whose life is in danger, we're getting out of here."

"But—!"

Ignoring her, Gray headed away from the ensnared vehicle and the mudslide. He focused all his energy and strength into hiking over slippery boulders while holding a 115-pound woman with an injury. Behind him, he half expected to hear the telltale sound of the old Jeep CJ being carried away down the mountain, but that sound never came.

Carrying her solid but small form, he reached the road she'd been driving on when she'd hit the mud. He couldn't imagine how terrifying that must have been. She was in her twenties, he'd guess, a few years younger than his thirty-two years. Was she a volunteer who he would work with? He'd have to explain what he'd been doing out here. But first they had to get somewhere safe and dry.

He hadn't made it twenty yards when the rain slowed.

"You can put me down now."

"You sure?"

She nodded. "I appreciate the help, but I can manage from here."

He set her on the still-slick road and put his hand out, ready to catch her if necessary. "Careful now."

Pushing her wet strands out of the way, she looked up at him, studying his face with her bright hazel eyes. Raindrops slid over her forehead and over her cheeks, revealing a pretty, natural face with a few freckles across the bridge of her nose and cheeks. Her dark hair hung long down her back and was so waterlogged that he couldn't tell for sure what color it was, but he was almost certain it was dark brown to match her perfectly shaped eyebrows.

He glanced up at the ashen sky and received droplets in his eyes. He wiped them out and then looked at the woman. "I suppose I should introduce myself. It's not every day I carry a woman down the mountain."

"I'm *walking* down the mountain," she corrected. "But I'm sure it's not every day you have to pull a woman trapped in a mud-strapped, tree-slammed Jeep."

"You got that right."

"Well, what's your name, stranger?"

"Grayson Wilson. But you can call me Gray." Though working undercover, he'd keep his first name. Easy enough to answer to that. Wilde would be off the books.

"I'm Gemma Rollins. I run Tiger Mountain, the sanctuary on the other side of this road. You might have noticed it since you were out wandering the area." Her tone sounded suspicious.

Gemma Rollins. Tiger Mountain's founder.

So much for his surveillance efforts. He should have known, though she looked nothing like the pictures, where she always had on sunglasses. Her eyes would have been a dead giveaway.

She shifted her focus to the road and then turned to him. "Well, are you coming? I want to get someplace dry."

"And then you'll call the sheriff, right?" The county maintained the mountain road, and she might want the report for her insurance.

Calling the sheriff was the right move for her, so Gray ignored the twinge he felt at the thought. Gray hadn't wanted to run into the man so soon on this operation, but Sheriff Kruse would likely send a deputy out instead and, in that case, Gray could keep his cover unless it was Deputy Callahan. In theory, it would be safe enough to read in the local cops on his investigation…but in practice, it was a whole different story. Sometimes, even law enforcement could be involved in trafficking.

"Yes. We need to let the county know about the mud and trees on the road."

She continued to favor her right leg over her left.

Gray asked, "Are you sure you're not hurt? You're limping."

Gemma stopped and turned to look at him, staring at him with her determined and enormous, crystal-clear hazel eyes. Why hadn't he known about the eyes beforehand?

Like that would have kept them from affecting him now. He didn't want to stop looking at them.

"I was injured years ago. Nerve damage. My limp is part of me now. If you had let me grab my cane out of the Jeep, I'd be using that to walk."

Gray was embarrassed. Why hadn't he noticed a cane in the few pictures he'd seen? "I'm so sorry. I didn't know." He almost offered to assist her in walking, but the set of her jaw told him that would be the wrong thing to do.

"It's okay. I understand. You were being a hero, and you couldn't have known you were rescuing a debilitated damsel. Honestly, I didn't expect anyone to hear my cries for help, much less a stranger to arrive to whisk me out of the Jeep. Thank you for that." Her soft smile wiped away the furrow in her brow but not the anguish—the deep-seated agony—behind her eyes.

Gray had come here to bring this woman down

if she was involved in the trafficking ring—and especially if she was involved, even indirectly, in Bill's death. It seemed more than likely that she was part of the trafficking ring as founder of the sanctuary that was somehow connected.

How could she not be aware of the trafficking going on right under her nose? But looking at her now, Gray doubted his certainty. He could clearly see there was so much more going on in that head of hers. Finding answers would not be as easy as he'd hoped.

Especially when his natural drive to protect the innocent ignited for Gemma. Because if she wasn't involved in the ring, then she could be in danger.

All he knew was that he had a feeling Gemma Rollins had just reversed their roles and she was about to make trouble for Gray. Either that or he had just made a world of trouble for himself in coming here.

TWO

Gemma kept up the warm and friendly banter while she shared the mountain road with Gray. She appreciated his assistance out of the CJ. She could have died without Gray's help.

But she kept the conversation superficial. Gray was still a stranger and she didn't know what he could have been doing on the mountain or on the road during this storm. She had even more reason to be wary given the saboteurs who had caused her too many problems already in the form of vandalism to the property. They hoped to sabotage her efforts to provide a reputable sanctuary for tigers. Could Gray be connected to them? It was certainly possible.

Pain throbbed up her leg, pain that seemed to ignite in full force when she was stressed in any way. And with all the stress in her life lately, that meant a lot of over-the-counter painkillers. She'd managed so far without prescription painkillers and wouldn't start now, if she could help it.

She must have flinched because she saw him eyeing her with concern. "So what happened back there, anyway?" he asked. "You come around that curve too fast? Or was it the muddy deluge in the road that took you out?"

Gemma scoffed. "Let's just say it was the perfect storm. My steering went out and the brakes couldn't handle the slope." She didn't want to go on, fearing he might berate her for her lack of vehicle maintenance. She tried to ignore that gnawing in the back of her mind that it was something more threatening.

His demeanor changed—a subtle shift, but it was there.

Gemma shouldn't have revealed so much. "I know, I know. Vintage doesn't have to be unsafe."

He cracked a grin.

Gray might be a stranger on this mountain, but he elicited a smile from her in return. She glanced at him. Covered in mud, he was kind of scruffy-looking, his hair hanging to his shoulders and making him resemble a character in an epic fantasy movie. He'd been there, right when she'd needed him. But…she was itching to ask what he'd been doing on the road.

Gemma wished she wasn't a conspiracy theorist. Hoped that she was being entirely too suspicions, but she'd been through so much already. And where was this guy's vehicle? Either something didn't add up or Gemma didn't have all the information necessary to fill in the equation. She suspected the first but hoped for the latter.

A vicious cramp shot pain up her leg and Gemma slipped and fell, letting out a yelp.

Humiliation scoured her. If not for her limp, she wouldn't have gone down. Pebbles and rocks bit into her backside, adding to the mud already there.

Gray whisked her up and into his arms before she could protest. The concern in his face, the compassion in his warm brown eyes, told her she had nothing to fear from him. But she had never trusted her own judgment when it came to men like Gray—handsome men, whom Gemma could be attracted to if she let herself. Fortunately, her single-minded focus on her work meant she hadn't run into that many men like Gray. Warmth spread through her as she rested in his arms and against his broad chest, or was the warmth from the embarrassment of her fall?

He grinned, though the distant rumble of trouble boiled in his gaze. "It's okay, Gemma. I'm handy to have around at times like these."

The guy made her laugh, easing her humiliation. "I see that."

"And I know my timing is off, but—" he cleared his throat "—it's about time for my interview. You want to interview me here and now or wait until we get to headquarters?"

Huh?

He must have noticed her bewilderment because he laughed. "I'm interested in your volunteer position."

Gemma slapped her hand onto her head. "Oh! Oh, this is…well…put me down now."

Without argument, he set her on her feet. "I'm just trying to show that I can be useful as a volunteer."

Through the woods, Gemma spotted the main sprawl of buildings. "We're close. Let's get inside, dry off and warm up, and we'll talk about volunteer work over a hot cup of cocoa. Is that all right?"

"Sounds perfect." He flashed a nice set of teeth.

At least she had a reason to hope that he wasn't connected with the saboteurs now. It didn't make sense that someone would volunteer to help her if he really wanted to hurt someone. But the thought caused a shadow in her heart. She didn't want that to be the case for Gray Wilson. She could ask any hard questions—What he was doing on the road? Where was his vehicle?—once they were inside with the others. But she didn't want to think he was up to no good. His actions had proven otherwise so far.

Gemma led him through the side door of the main facility they hoped to open up for public education and training in the next few weeks. "This is the resource building. There's a big fire roaring in the fireplace for days like this. So have a seat. I'll get you a towel to dry off and a blanket to get warm."

The faux leather couches could be wiped clean of mud and debris.

She disappeared down a hall toward her office, where she found Cara, her friend and employee, busy working on the computer recording data for the tigers and ordering supplies.

She glanced up at Gemma and gasped. "What happened?"

"It's a long story. I have a guy out there, Gray Wilson, who says he was coming in for an interview today?"

Cara nodded. "Yeah. I left a message on your voice mail. He called this morning, and you said you needed help and, well, I thought you'd be back in time."

"I met him on the mountain."

"What?"

"Yeah. I crashed the CJ into a tree. Gray was there to help me out."

"Oh, Gemma, are you okay, honey? Do you need to see a doctor?"

"No, I'm good."

Cara didn't look convinced. "What about that old Jeep you love? You want me to call the sheriff for you? You'll need an official report so insurance will cover it."

"It's not like the insurance is going to pay." She only had liability. "But call the county to let them know about the road."

She dried her hair with one of the towels they kept on hand. Their work at the sanctuary was hands on, dirty work. Grabbing a couple of blankets from a closet, Gemma wrapped one around herself, wishing she had time to run over to her cabin to shower, change clothes and grab a sweatshirt. "Find my other cane for me, if you would, please? I don't want to keep him waiting."

Cara nodded. "I'll find it."

"Well, I'm off to see if we can use him."

But Gemma already knew the answer. He was definitely sturdy and able. But she was more curious about his background and what brought him to Tiger Mountain than anything.

She made her way to Gray, who stood by the fire, and offered him the blanket. "Wrap this around you. I can offer you coffee or hot chocolate."

He was indecisive behind his frown. "I don't want to trouble you."

"I'm getting some for myself, so it's no trouble."

"Then let me do it for you."

"Mr. Wilson, you're not a volunteer here yet. You're my guest. Now, would you like some or not?"

"Hot chocolate's fine. And…please call me Gray."

The mundane act of getting hot chocolate let Gemma compose her thoughts and settle her heart after wrecking the CJ and being carried by a stranger. Blanket still hanging on her shoulders, Gemma carried two cups of hot cocoa out to where Gray waited, hoping he would not look at her leg. There wasn't anything to see, really. Not like it was hideous or mangled. Instead it was stiff and aching.

She tried to smile to cover the pain. He'd settled on the big old orange couch next to the fire and appeared mesmerized by the flames, deep in thought. Good, he hadn't watched her limping walk.

"Here you go."

Slowly he turned his head to her, seeming to shake off his daze. "Thanks."

She handed the mug off. Of course their fingers brushed. But Gemma had already been up close and personal with Gray, so she didn't understand the current she suddenly felt. She wondered what he might look like when he was all cleaned up. Where had that come from? *Ignore, ignore, ignore.* "Well, we're off to an awkward start."

He quirked a brow and flashed a dimpled half grin. "At least it wasn't uneventful."

Gemma's heart hammered again at the reminder. At least she thought it was the reminder of her crash that elevated her heart rate and not his dimpled grin.

His smile suddenly dropped away. "I shouldn't have made a joke about it. You could have died. It could have been much worse."

Shaking her head slightly, she slurped in the warm cocoa. This was definitely what she needed. Get her core temperature back up and her brain working. It might be spring in southwest Oregon, but the rain dropped cold in the mountains.

"It worked out because you were there, at the right place at the right time. You've proven that you're physically strong enough to handle working for us, but tell me about your background—who are you, where do you come from, why do you want to volunteer and what experience do you have with animals, specifically big cats?"

"That's a lot of questions in one breath."

Gemma was botching the interview, but it all came rushing out and then she let the one question burning her mind spill.

"And why were you on the mountain today?" It wasn't like he'd simply shown up for an interview early. He'd been on the sanctuary property up in the mountains. The thought made her bristle.

Whoa with all the questions at once. But at least he'd anticipated them, even her last one. He had thought of an answer for that one while she'd gone to get the blankets. He hadn't expected for anyone to see him on the mountain or to rescue Gemma from a Jeep.

Without hesitation, he said, "I parked my truck where the county road meets Highway 101 and then hiked in. I was early for the interview and like to see the lay of the land where I'm going to work." It was as simple as that. And completely truthful. "Or, um…volunteer. But whether I'm salaried or not, I always take my work seriously."

"But you were on private property."

"Actually, I wasn't. I was still in the Wild Rogue Wilderness when I heard your cries for help. Only then did I cross over onto your property." Sure, he'd been checking the tigers and facilities from a distance with a set of binoculars—left behind when he'd run after her. Still, by the look on her face, he might have said too much.

She cocked a brow. "Getting the lay of the land, huh?"

Time to switch the topic. "I recently rented a house on the coast from a friend. I wanted a change of scenery from my place in Portland. I have a biology degree and worked in wildlife conservation before. I know that tigers are the most imperiled of the wild cats. Three subspecies are already extinct. There's only about three thousand left, living in the wild."

She arched a brow. Impressed? Or maybe he was trying too hard. He needed this volunteer position. But he couldn't let her see just how much.

"It's because I believe in what you're doing that I wanted to volunteer my time while I'm between contracts. It makes me angry when I read about the dwindling endangered species populations and abused animals. You're doing a good thing here. I believe in your cause." Okay, now he was repeating himself. His pulse was beginning to roar in his ears. He'd better shut this down or he'd go off again and she would think he was too crazy to keep around.

But he didn't have to worry as he saw the suspicion drain from her face. And all because he said he believed in her cause.

She limped closer to the fire and, without thinking, he offered a hand. "Are you sure you're okay?" Then remembered she'd said her limp was part of her now. She didn't want his help. "Since you were in an accident today, maybe you should see a doctor."

Her look silenced him on the matter. "I've already told you what happened. The reason for my limp." She bent over to stoke the fire, her long hair hanging down.

"You didn't, actually. Just that you had an injury. How did it happen?"

"I was in another car wreck." She straightened up. A distant look came into her eyes.

"I'm sorry to hear that."

Gray almost tossed out a joke about her skills as a driver but thought better of it. As she stood by the fire to warm up, her eyes grew bright, flames dancing in them. He'd never seen anyone more alive than Gemma Rollins. And she truly seemed to be passionate about sheltering the abused wildlife and caring for them. Yet someone at this sanctuary was involved in crimes against the tigers. To use a sanctuary as a cover for trafficking was about as low as a person could go in Gray's opinion. Was there any chance someone else was behind the trafficking? Who would have the authority or access to do so without Gemma noticing? The simplest answer was the one he didn't want to believe—that she was involved in the trafficking after all. He could hardly believe the conflicting emotions she stirred in him. But it was time for him to push them aside and get to know the real Gemma Rollins and what she was really up to with the sanctuary.

"Thanks. It happened a long time ago." With a frown she refocused on him. "What do you do,

Gray, when you're not volunteering? You mentioned you're between contracts."

"I'm a computer programming whiz."

She angled her head, confusion in her eyes.

He chuckled. "I know what you're thinking. I have a biology degree and I'm a computer whiz? As it turns out, learning to code is an important skill for biologists or any other science field, especially those who spend most of their time crunching data. I had a heads up on that skill. Growing up, I spent too much time playing video games and ended up learning to code early on as a side hobby. Though when I wasn't playing games, the rest of the time I was outdoors, exploring nature. I love animals, and I want to do something meaningful with my life." There. He hadn't even had to lie to keep his cover. He was currently working on installing new accounting software for Wilderness, Inc., a wilderness survival training company run by his brother, Cooper, though he'd had to put that aside temporarily to investigate Tiger Mountain.

Gray was only a silent partner at Wilderness, Inc. anyway. He invested in the business but didn't want to make decisions or be involved in running the place.

He'd been at the Wilderness, Inc. office in Gideon when he'd received the tip about Tiger Mountain. With this new tip, he believed he was close to solving this case, and he was geographically close as well.

Gemma sat on the sofa and he did the same, across from her. She studied him over the rim of her cup of hot chocolate.

Gray shrugged. "Any more questions?"

"Nope. You have any for me?"

Yep. I have plenty of questions. But he had to be careful and ask the simple questions a volunteer, a wildlife enthusiast, would ask.

"I'm a hands-on kind of guy. I like to learn the ropes as I work. So any questions I have for you can be answered while I'm working. Oh, well, I guess there is one question. You going to let me volunteer or not?"

She gave him her soft and simple smile, the same one he'd seen on the road. It kindled a feeling he hadn't experienced in a long time and he didn't want to feel that again. He'd have to be careful around Gemma.

"You're hired," she said.

A woman appeared from the hallway and came over to them. Gemma introduced Cara as a Tiger Mountain employee. She handed a cane to Gemma. "Found it."

Gemma's faced colored. She'd said that her limp was part of her, but she didn't appear that comfortable with it. "Maybe I can get my other one from the CJ, if it's even salvageable."

Gray glanced out the window, noting the rain had finally and completely stopped. How long that would last, he didn't know. "Mind if I start work today? You can give me a tour of the place and show me what you need me for later, but right now maybe I can get your Jeep down the mountain."

Her eyes went even brighter. "Are you serious?"

"Sure, if you have a truck with a winch around here. Or, if not, we can call a wrecker, but I'll take care of it. You can get back to doing what's important." Gray found that, despite his true reason for being at Tiger Mountain, he honestly wanted to be useful to Gemma. But he reminded himself he wasn't here for her. He was working undercover to expose illegal activities at Tiger Mountain.

Gemma gave him the go-ahead and introduced him to Tom, a full-time staffer who had a four-wheel drive with a winch, which came in handy at a big cat sanctuary. Gray rode with Tom so he could show him where the vehicle had ended up.

Tom slowed the truck when they came to the mud slick in the road. A chunk of mountain seemed to have slid across the way. Tom sighed. "Gemma is not going to like this. Not one bit. She's already had a tough time here. I tell you, if it's not one thing, it's another."

Gray wanted to ask Tom more about what troubles Gemma had, but they were here. "This is where her CJ went into the tree. If you look to your left and up a bit, you'll see it just over the rise."

"I can see the bumper from here and hopefully the rest is still attached."

"Only one way to find out." When Gray stepped onto the road, his thoughts reverted to saving Gemma, holding her against him and hiking over the rocks and road.

He remembered her mentioning the perfect storm, her brakes quitting during the drive while the power steering had gone out as well. She would have shifted to the lowest gear, no doubt, and possibly tried the parking brake, but going down a steep mountain road would have worked against her. Even if it hadn't been raining and even without a mudslide, that could have been deadly. The Jeep CJ rested right where he'd left it, only it was steeped in thick, clotting mud. The vehicle was decades old and the brake hose was likely just as ancient and could have given out. But the steering, too, on the same day?

In such situations, he often referred to Occam's Razor, a principle of philosophy—the simplest explanation was the right one—and in this case, the chance that both the brakes and the steering went out at the same time on their own was unlikely. In which case he wanted to get a closer look. Had the vehicle been sabotaged?

Tigers were worth more dead than alive, their parts bringing money in excess of a hundred grand, thanks to the demand for traditional Asian medicine. All it took was finding a buyer on the black market and someone needing money could easily make it in spades.

Gemma Rollins might be standing in the way of that. If Gray discovered her life was in danger, he would not only work undercover, but serve as her protector.

THREE

Gemma exited the shower, glad to finally be free of the grime and mud. But she wished she could shake the disquiet the crash had left her with. The sun had finally set and she'd hurried home—a cabin across from the main facilities—to clean up. Tom had texted that he and Gray had been able to get her CJ to Carl's body shop.

With the Jeep taken care of for now, she had the freedom to focus her energies elsewhere—such as on her wish list, which was more like a needs list for the sanctuary. Two-way radios for everyone went on the top of the list. If Gray hadn't showed up, radios would have come in handy. They didn't require a cell signal and would provide essential communication with the habitats so spread out. She wrote that down.

She had so many hopes and dreams for making Tiger Mountain great to build a legacy and fulfill the dreams her parents had for a big cat sanctuary. Dreams that had been dashed when they'd died in a plane crash, and ultimately, with her uncle's death after that.

And this time, Gemma would not allow rumors of abuse to spoil their reputation. Her parents had not exploited the animals and endangered their sanctuary status by putting the cats on display or allowing pictures to be taken with the animals. Or people to pet the cubs because they had no cubs. They were not breeding the animals! Nor had they abused the animals by underfeeding them.

Still those rumors had destroyed their donor base and her parents were returning from a trip to meet with an investor who could revive their private foundation that supported Tiger Hills when their plane had crashed.

She'd never understood why someone had started the rumors.

Or who.

But after their death, her uncle had worked tirelessly to hold things together under great pressure. After the car accident in which he died, and with Gemma in the hospital undergoing multiple surgeries, there had been no one left to manage Tiger Hills or answer the untrue rumors of abuse that continued. The rumors meant donors fell away and without funding to keep the animals fed, the rumors would become true.

There had been no funding left to even pay for staff, and she didn't want the possibility that a full-scale investigation would further humiliate her family so she didn't stand in the way when the powers-that-be removed the animals and transferred them to other sanctuaries while she remained in the hospital.

Gemma spent several debilitated months going through two surgeries for her leg. She'd been devastated, broken both physically and emotionally over her losses. But once she was free to think about her future, she went to Oregon State University, got her conservation biology degree and masters in nonprofit management with the help of a financial grant and student loans, and planned for the day when she could start all over. Building something new and untainted as a way of restoring all that was lost to her family.

Her father had started Tiger Hill one tiger at a time when she was only five. Ten years later, he'd died in a plane crash. At twenty-eight, building a new sanctuary was the only way Gemma could think to get back the only life she'd ever known.

The process of creating a nonprofit foundation to support the new sanctuary, all the paperwork and certifications, building new enclosures and creating protocols, hiring staff and finding volunteers had taken several years. Once they'd met the licensing requirements, they starting acquiring the animals. Now with all their animals in place, they were ready for the USDA inspection—she was that close to realizing her dream.

She had seven people to help, including Gray. With fifteen tigers to care for, she wanted three more people to even out the workload. With a high turnover rate lately, was that even possible?

Clyde, her father and uncle's longtime friend, seemed to think so. She'd understood him to be a silent partner in the old sanctuary, but he'd been out of the country involved with his conservation organization during the time of their deaths. She hadn't seen him since she was very young, but he'd come to her rescue and invested a lot of money into her project of opening a new sanctuary. He was all she had left now—well, that and Tiger Mountain.

From her cabin across from the Tiger Mountain facilities, Gemma could hear one of the tigers roar. Their roars could be heard up to two miles away. She didn't understand why Emil Atkins, the rancher whose property ran next to the sanctuary, found the tiger sounds disconcerting. Maybe it was more that his horses and cattle were disturbed, spurring him to lobby against the sanctuary, stirring up the other rural neighbors and ranchers.

Personally, Gemma found the sounds useful, since they let her know when something was upsetting one of the tigers. Maybe someone tampered with the cages, disturbing her tigers.

Or maybe it was more vandalism.

Irritation prickled the back of her neck.

Maybe it was Emil. Gemma needed to check. Grabbing a jacket, she paused to stare out the window into the pitch black of night. She couldn't see a thing. The sense that someone watched her crawled over her. Reaching for the drapes to pull them shut, she paused when lightning flashed in the distance and thunder followed, rumbling through Gemma's core.

Before she could close the drapes, someone knocked on the door, startling her.

She calmed her pounding heart and rushed to the door. A quick glance through the peephole into the darkness revealed nothing. Gemma flipped on the porch light.

Gray Wilson.

She frowned. What did he want?

Gemma opened the door. He'd cleaned himself up and wore jeans and a light black jacket over a blue polo shirt. His shaggy hair was neat and combed. She held back her smile. A gust of wind blew in and carried the scent of soap. He smelled nice too. "Gray, what brings you here?"

His expression grew somber. "Mind if I come in for a minute?"

"Actually, I was on my way out to check on the tigers. Heard one of them roaring."

"Another storm's approaching. Can't it wait?"

"What? Afraid of getting wet again?" She teased him, but the concern in his eyes increased her sense of uneasiness.

"We need to talk." He grabbed her arm and guided her inside. Oddly enough, his action didn't scare or offend her but confirmed the seriousness of the situation.

Suddenly, the room seemed too dark.

Gemma flicked on a lamp. "What is it, Gray?"

"While the Jeep was propped up on the wrecker, I took a look underneath. You mentioned the brakes and the steering went out at the same time. That's unusual enough that I wanted to tinker. Look a little harder."

Goosebumps rose on her arms. "And?"

"I think someone tampered with your brakes."

Gemma stiffened. She'd been on suspicion overload and hadn't wanted to think about that possibility. But she held on to the hope that he was wrong. "What makes you the expert? If the mechanic didn't see it?"

"I helped my dad restore an old hot rod and a few other vehicles. I know my way around cars."

"That still doesn't explain why you would find it and the mechanic wouldn't." She wanted to remain in denial. Find a reason he could be mistaken.

"Carl's a nice guy, but he gave it a passing glance. I didn't, that's all. Nor did I point it out to him."

Interesting. "Because…?"

"Because someone worked hard to make this look like an accident. And they might lash out or get desperate if word spreads that you know it wasn't. But I think you should call the sheriff about this—discreetly. Someone tampered with your brakes. Knew that they would be completely out by the time you were swerving around the dangerous bends in the mountain road. I would have called him myself, but I left that up to you. It's your business."

"And the steering? Anybody tamper with that? With no brakes and no real way to steer, I should have gone right over the edge." Then she allowed the truth she'd wanted to ignore to sink in. Gemma was sitting on the sofa before she even realized it. *Somebody tried to kill me?*

"No." Gray huffed a laugh. "The steering was just shot. That was just unfortunate." Gray frowned.

A chill crawled up her spine and around her throat. Gemma pressed her hand to her neck. When Gray took a step toward her, she instinctively stood from the couch and stepped around it, putting the furniture between her and Gray Wilson. It had been sheer chance that her steering had failed—and then sheer chance that she'd survived. That she'd been able to keep the Jeep from going over the road. That she'd screamed for help and someone had come. Chance…or was it? He had appeared out of nowhere today.

She studied him even as he watched her. Had he been the one to tamper with her brakes? He would have had to follow her up the mountain. Done his work while she'd left the Jeep alone. He'd definitely had the opportunity. But what about motive? Why do that only to save her?

"You were conveniently on the mountain today." What was she doing? She shouldn't accuse him right here and now, but she had to know. And in her heart of hearts, she didn't believe he would do such a thing. But if not Gray, then who?

"What? You think…" Gray threw up his hands. "You think I did that? I don't even know you. And if I wanted you to crash, why would I try to save you or tell you someone tampered with the vehicle and that you should call the sheriff to start an investigation?"

"Why indeed." To gain her confidence? Gemma scraped her hands through her hair. "I'm sorry. I know it sounds absurd, but I had to bring it up. You know the sheriff will."

Gray tensed. "Yeah, he'll ask if you bring it up."

"I won't have to. He'll want to know about

anyone new who is working on the sanctuary." Gemma looked again out the window.

"Just anyone new? Why's that?"

"He's already looked into anyone who has been here longer than two months. Checking on the neighbors too."

"Why? What aren't you telling me?"

"I didn't want to scare you off so soon. There have been a few happenings."

"Happenings?"

"Up to now, it's just been vandalism and a little petty theft." She hadn't wanted to get into this with Gray before he even had a chance to meet the tigers and fall in love with them. "There are a few people around who don't want the sanctuary to succeed. So, once in a while, we have trouble. Vandalism that amounts to sabotage." *Please don't ask me more...*

"But do you think they would go so far as to try to kill you?"

"No. I can't believe that. Or, at least, I couldn't until just now. I don't...I don't know anymore. And I don't know why you would care so much."

Gray closed the drapes for her. "I'm just a volunteer who happened to show up on the day someone tried to kill you, Gemma. I want to help you—keep you from getting hurt. And that's why I'm telling you that you need to call the sheriff. And be on your guard. Keep your blinds and curtains drawn. And keep your head about you. Be careful around strangers."

Gray Wilson was a stranger to her, so it seemed odd he would say that, though it was good advice. He arched a brow.

"And be even more vigilant around people you know."

Gray watched Gemma's reaction to his warning.

Wariness lurked behind her gaze. Lightning flashed again and thunder sounded as though it was on top of them.

"I didn't mean to scare you by telling you about the brakes. But you needed to know."

"I'm not sure whether to thank you or not." She gave a nervous laugh and then released a long sigh.

Through a cracked window, he heard the tiger roar. Gemma glanced over, apparently still worried about the big cats—maybe even more than she worried about herself. That could be dangerous, but he admired her dedication.

"Why don't you wait to go out there until the worst of the storm passes? I'll go see the tigers with you. After all, that's what I volunteered for." He grinned, hoping to lighten the mood.

She smiled in return, appearing to relax. The only trouble was Gray didn't want her to relax too much. She needed to take the brake tampering seriously. Gray hoped the sheriff encouraged her in that. He'd met Sheriff Kruse but didn't know him as well as Cooper did. He hoped that the sheriff was a man who could be trusted. Gray didn't think anyone in local law enforcement was involved, but there was no way to know for sure—that was why it was so important that his cover remain intact, so he'd have to be conveniently absent when the sheriff showed up. And while working undercover, he could do a little investigating into the saboteurs she'd mentioned and anyone else who might want the sanctuary to fail. More importantly, he needed to learn why someone would want Gemma dead.

Were the vandalism and the attempt on her life connected? The two acts seemed different enough that they could be from two different people. Gray had a friend—a forensic investigator—who might be able to offer advice on the profiles of who might be behind these two very different crimes.

But first, he'd need to ask her what sort of things the saboteurs had done. Why the sheriff hadn't stopped them. But then he'd come across as an investigator. Besides, the way she shivered and hugged herself, he wanted to dial down the fear and tension. He needed to gain her confidence before he moved too fast.

He had taken a step out of his role as a nobody volunteer in coming to her cabin. In making the disclosure about her brakes. Maybe it would have suited his purposes better to keep the information to himself to see what developed, but he had a moral and ethical obligation to let her know what kind of danger she was potentially in.

"We can head over to the resource building while we wait. Get the keys for one of the utility vehicles. It's quicker to get in and out," she said.

"I guess now would be a good time for you to give me that tour I never got today."

"Maybe. Except it's dark out. You can't see everything. But, yeah, I can show you some things."

Gray followed Gemma, who was ably walking with her cane, noting she hadn't locked her door. "Aren't you going to lock up?"

She paused, turned to face him. "What? No... I—"

"You don't usually lock up?"

She shook her head. "Never had a reason to."

"Until now. You are taking me seriously, aren't you?"

Frowning, she headed into the house and returned with keys and locked the door. "There. Satisfied?"

"Yes."

She headed toward the main building. Gray caught up to her in two long strides. "I know it's kind of awkward and all. First I pull you from the wreckage and carry you across a mudslide to safety only to learn that you're the woman I'm supposed to interview with. And now I show up at your cabin and tell you someone tampered with your brakes. Believe me, it's weird for me too."

"I'll admit it's a lot to happen in one day." Gemma paused beneath the security light on the porch of the main office and tried the door. It didn't open, and she jingled the keys. "Good thing I went back for them. Someone locked up."

"I hope that's the usual practice."

"It is—I'd just lost track of the time, or I would have remembered to grab the keys in the first place. Wouldn't do to have computers or paperwork stolen."

"Especially with the saboteurs running around."

"Exactly."

"But you're not worried about your cabin."

"No, I wasn't. Not until you showed up tonight. I didn't think they would go that far. I don't keep anything of real value in the cabin."

Once inside, Gemma grabbed a set of keys out of a key box and then led him out the side door to a commercial carport, where two utility vehicles— old Gators—were parked along with some other equipment. Gemma had a thing for old equipment, it seemed. Either that or limited funding.

"You could use a fence around this to make sure nobody steals this equipment."

"It's on my wish list. I'm making a list to give to the man who helped me establish the private foundation and funded most of it to get Tiger Mountain up and running—Clyde Morris. He's been out of town. Out of the country, rather, but he'll be here tomorrow and I need to be ready with the list. At some point, I won't have to depend on him so much. We're working on building our donor base but it takes time."

His pulse hiked up.

Clyde Morris.

Gray was definitely listening. Could this be the guy he was after? A single primary funder was unusual for an expensive operation like this one. The man had to have some reason for investing so heavily in the tiger sanctuary. Was it so he could use the animals for his smuggling? Gray knew better than to jump to conclusions—but it was still a lead worth following. "Why don't you tell me what's happened? You keep mentioning someone is trying to sabotage the sanctuary."

Ignoring him, Gemma grabbed a couple of flashlights and climbed into the utility vehicle. "You coming or what?"

"I thought we were going to wait for the storm."

"I think it's a lot of noise and threats. It might

not even rain, and I don't have all night. I need to check on that tiger."

After Gray got in, he held on when she took off. She might struggle to walk and need a cane, but she had no trouble driving or shifting gears. That made him smile. "Well, tell me more about the issues. As a volunteer, I should know. You're not really afraid you're going to scare me off, are you?"

Waiting for her answer, he studied her profile. At least a few security lights had been installed at strategic points.

She glanced over at him. "You got me."

"Really? I was only joking."

"I've already lost an intern and two volunteers over this stuff."

Wow. "Look, Gemma. I'm a big boy. I can handle anything you have to say. Anything you think is going to happen. In fact, I'll go so far as to say maybe I'm supposed to be here to protect you. Keep you safe."

The Gator slammed to a stop, almost sending Gray flying. He jerked his head to Gemma. Had she done that on purpose? Gemma hopped from the vehicle, holding a flashlight. He followed her down the paved trail and she let them in through a gated fence—the first enclosure to surround the sanctuary, nesting two more fenced areas, he noticed. She unlocked and opened the gate to yet another fenced area.

"We have twenty main habitats the animals have access to. Each habitat has a lot of space with trees and grass, rocks and a pool. All the habitats connect to indoor buildings with stalls—four habitats to each of the indoor buildings. We call the indoor buildings Habitats A, B, C, D and E. Five buildings total. We have fifteen cats right now, but eventually, I hope to add more."

She led him down the path that wove through well-kept grounds with large secured areas. He saw now why her vehicles were old. She put all her money into the habitats and care of the animals. "During the day, the tigers are locked outside in their habitats while we clean the holding areas. I need your help with all of it. The cleaning, the feeding. We have an older cat, Caesar, who requires special care and takes extra time. I know it doesn't seem like much, but with so many cats and so few people it can be exhausting. And dealing with the daily maintenance has put me behind on administrative tasks. I have to work on proposals and grants and educating the public and most importantly getting ready for the upcoming USDA inspection. We have to always be prepared for surprise inspections, as well, but it's all I can do to take care of the big cats."

She looked at him, waiting for his reaction, he

supposed. He shrugged. "I'm good with anything you throw at me. Lead on."

Gemma walked in front of him, and he couldn't help but notice that, with her cane, she had a gentle, rolling gait, almost like a tiger.

"At night, they have full access to their habitats, both inside and out."

Gray stopped to watch as a tiger he could barely see in the dark disappeared inside. "Do all the habitats have these multilevel platforms and pools?"

"Yep. We don't want the cats getting bored. We also rotate them so they are able to explore new habitats every few days. Wouldn't want them to get bored or start pacing like you see in zoos."

"You're encouraging them toward naturalistic behaviors."

She smiled. "You sound like a press kit. How are you at public speaking?"

He shrugged. "Okay, I guess. Why do you ask?"

"I could use help educating the public about what we're doing here. I want them to know why the cats need this place. I want to teach everyone about the endangerments the big cats face in the wild and in captivity. And about poaching and trafficking."

"Now *that* I can do." He wondered if he sounded a little too eager, too knowledgeable about the topic that was the basis of his career.

But Gemma had no reason to suspect he was a special agent investigating Tiger Mountain, unless, of course, she was guilty.

Gemma led him deeper into the sanctuary, the moon finally filtering through the storm clouds and casting odd, dappled shadows through the refuge. Would it rain or not? Gemma still used her flashlight to chase away the shadows, and, by the way she continually shined the light into the dark corners, he knew she was taking his warnings seriously. Or her wariness could have to do with the vandalism, whatever trouble the saboteurs had been causing for her.

Finally they came upon a habitat with a pacing tiger and when the growl came, Gray knew this tiger was the one causing the ruckus. Pausing at the cage, Gemma sighed. "This is Kayla. She came from El Paso where she was chained in a too-small concrete cage for a roadside attraction at a truck stop. Someone bred tigers there too and sold the cubs to people who stopped in to get gas. She's usually very calm. Something's disturbed her."

He heard the frustration in her voice and more—she expected to find something wrong, such as more vandalism. Gemma walked the perimeter of the enclosure, shining her flashlight around.

Gray kept up with her, leaning in close to whisper. "I'm thinking now would be a good time to tell me what you're expecting to find. What has someone been doing to scare you like this?"

She gasped and jumped into him, dropping the flashlight. "That. That's what I'm looking for." Gemma pointed at something inside the habitat.

"Stay back." Gray grabbed the flashlight and pushed her behind him, not having a clue what she'd seen.

Then he found it. What was it, exactly? His mind was slow to wrap around it.

"It's a doll. Supposed to be me, slashed up and covered with blood."

Frowning, Gray shook his head, wishing he could have removed the doll before Gemma had seen it. But, considering her certainty after just one look, he realized she'd seen this kind of thing before. What he didn't know was if the person or persons responsible also had murder on their mind.

His first impression of her—that she was about to make trouble for him—had been all wrong. No. Gemma Rollins wasn't making trouble.

She was *in* trouble. In deep.

FOUR

"Is this the sort of thing that has your staff and volunteers leaving?"

"Yes and no. The attacks aren't always so…creative." This had her skin crawling, even though it wasn't the first of its kind. She used the clicker she kept in her pocket, signaling Kayla to go inside and remain there. Though the sanctuary's purpose was to offer a natural environment, some training was required for the tigers to live in captivity.

She took the flashlight from him and shined it around. "Looks like Kayla has gone inside. Now would be a good time to shut her in so we can get the doll out for evidence."

"Wait. Shouldn't we leave it like it is so the sheriff can see it?" Gray asked.

"You mean cordon it off as a crime scene and all that?" Gemma laughed. "That's exactly what they want so they can mess with my tigers. And by *they* I mean the neighboring ranchers. I'd have to shuffle the tigers around, disrupt the routine and I'd be short a habitat until Sheriff Kruse and his deputies could get to it. I'm almost of a mind not to call it in at all. Let them try to scare me. I'm not so easily scared."

A noise startled her. Gemma gasped. *Right. She's not so easily scared.* Sounded like a large object, maybe a garbage can, being knocked over. "Do you think whoever left this is still here?"

She started off toward the noise, but Gray grabbed her arm. "No. It's too dangerous. I would suggest waiting in the vehicle, but the Gator isn't going to provide any protection." He looked as if he wanted to run toward the sound himself but was visibly hesitating. "No way am I leaving you here alone."

While she was glad he didn't plan on leaving her, she hadn't exactly asked for his protection.

He hurried in the direction of the sound, leaving Gemma to keep up with him the best she could with a cane. Who was this guy anyway? Taking over like he owned the place. Gemma should be indignant, but Gray's actions kind of warmed her heart. Still, it didn't wash away her fury at the vandalism. Didn't these people realize the animals had already been abused in one way or another? They didn't need to be tormented anymore. Gemma followed Gray around a corner, watching as he flashed the beam of light with his own flashlight, searching the shadows while she hoped for a signal to call the sheriff's office on her cell. Finally, she got one and stood in place to keep it. She wondered what it meant that the number was saved on her phone.

She left a message with Laura, the dispatcher, about a new incident. Seeing an effigy of herself had only happened once before. Usually the trouble involved more mundane things like dismantling half the fence for a tiger's habitat or spray-painting vulgar words on the buildings. All of it was meant to wear her down. Didn't these people realize the extent of her commitment?

They found an overturned garbage can near a small utility building. Gray put his hand up. "Don't take another step." He flashed the light around the ground. "Maybe someone was here and left some tracks. The sheriff can use that."

"Whatever you say." She waited a beat. "See any yet?"

"It's too dark out. With all the rain of late and mud, though, we're bound to find a few."

"Right, but you're going to see tracks belonging to volunteers and staff as well."

"Has anyone been out here since the rain stopped this afternoon?"

"Of course. Tigers still need to be cared for. Things don't stop because it rains." She thought back to this afternoon. Well, maybe things do stop a little when you have an accident. That had thrown off her afternoon—and Tom's too, when he went to haul the Jeep into town. "Look, Gray, I appreciate you trying to turn all detective and everything, but I think finding a distinctive shoe print in this mud is a lost cause. Besides, Sheriff Kruse is already investigating. He could have his own list of suspects, but I think it's the rancher neighbors. None of them are happy that we're here. The most vocal has been Emil Atkins. He hasn't been shy about letting me know what he thinks about the sanctuary. He doesn't like it so close to his ranch. He's threatened me a few times, but they were idle threats. So now he's escalated to foolhardy attempts to scare me off."

The way Gray looked at her told Gemma he was thinking about her brakes.

"Once Sheriff Kruse hears about this, he'll send one of his deputies out here to get the doll for evidence. Then one of them will visit the ranchers and ask questions and throw a few warnings out. It's a game we've been playing for a long time."

She waited and watched his reaction with only the dim light of the distant security lamp illuminating his face. But his frown was easy to see. He looked up at the sky as though expecting to watch the stars but instead found disappointing darkness in the clouds that hadn't yet dumped their burden. How strange. Even stranger, Gemma could totally relate to that.

Finally, Gray dropped his gaze to her. "I'm sorry you're going through this, Gemma. I know we've only just met, and you don't know me, but I'm here to help if I can."

And Gemma believed him. That was the problem—she usually believed people, whether she should or not. Gemma had been such a poor judge of character, and she shouldn't rely on that inner sense that told her Gray was trustworthy.

"Let's go and get the effigy out of the habitat and then head back to the Gator so we can leave here." This made her sick, absolutely sick.

Once they were in the Gator and Kayla's habitat was effigy-free so the big cat could roam at will, Gray glanced at Gemma. "I'd really like to hear about the other incidents."

"I know, Gray, but I really don't want to talk about them right now, if that's all right. Besides, I didn't hire you to investigate or even protect me. I hired you to shovel manure, clean out habitats while the cats are outside and maybe, if you're a good speaker, help me educate the public and convince the neighbors that we are no danger to them."

Her tone was hard, she knew that, but he seemed to take it in stride, understanding her mood. She was somewhat surprised at his determination to stay after everything he'd seen. And yet, Gray Wilson was still here, eager to help.

But Gemma had a big question burning in her mind. A question she wasn't willing to voice and barely willing to think about. After losing her parents and her uncle, was Gemma willing to stay—to build Tiger Mountain and keep it thriving—in the face of warnings and threats on her life? Her greatest fear was that she wasn't strong enough to see it through, to build a new sanctuary to match or even surpass what her father had built years ago. But if she was strong enough to stay, she hoped to restore her family's reputation destroyed by vicious rumors.

Who had started them?

Gemma steered the Gator into the covered garage and parked, hating how her mood had soured.

"I'll walk you to your cabin."

"No need, really," she protested weakly. Gemma was too tired to fight him, if he persisted.

"Well, my truck is parked that way anyway." He grinned.

Gemma could easily grow to like that grin. But she didn't like it yet. No. Not yet.

He strolled next to her. "Listen, the big cats are important to you. I get that. But who's going to take care of the tigers if you don't care of yourself?"

At her porch, she turned to him. "What are you trying to say?"

"When the sheriff or a deputy comes tomorrow to get the effigy and dismiss it as just another childish prank, tell them about your brakes. Promise me?"

"I don't have to promise you, Gray." Why was he making this so personal? "But I'll tell him. I appreciate you thinking of the tigers."

And of me...

She nodded her goodbye and went inside her cabin. Shutting the door behind her, she leaned against it.

"Who's going to take care of the tigers if you don't take care of yourself, indeed?" She mumbled the question.

Why would someone try to kill her? It made no sense.

Her parents' tragic deaths had been followed by her uncle's just three short years later. Ten years later, Gemma was still haunted by the accident that killed Uncle Dave. Had his death been cold-blooded murder engineered to look like an accident?

At his temporary living quarters—the rental house on the beach—Gray tossed his keys on the table.

The accommodations were sparsely furnished

but served his purpose. At least it wasn't too close to Gideon, Oregon, where his siblings, Cooper and Alice, worked at Wilderness, Inc., providing excursions and survival training. If he was any closer, he feared he would run into someone who could give his true identity away. He had to keep his distance from Sheriff Kruse, as it was.

Still, he hadn't worked in southwest Oregon when he'd been a game warden, so he shouldn't run into too many people he knew, other than the sheriff's department. When he'd been offered the job with the federal government as a special agent with the USFWS, then he'd worked out of the Portland, Oregon, regional office and traveled throughout Pacific Northwest.

Now, Gray was a senior special agent hoping for a management position as a Resident Agent in Charge. That could mean a move to another regional office or even to headquarters in Falls Church, Virginia. The selection process was competitive and if Gray was promoted...well, maybe then Dad would be proud of him.

His stomach soured at the thought of his father. He thought he'd extricated that need for approval from his life. Gray had always believed he was the black sheep of the family until Jeremy committed suicide. Nothing compared to that. Still, Cooper was the son their dad was proud of. Not Gray.

He sighed and grabbed a soda from the fridge, noticing his cell buzzed.

Ten minutes later he finished a call with his superior, Mark Jenkins. Gray filled him in on the new developments. He hadn't come into this expecting to discover that someone was trying to kill Gemma.

Why had the mechanic been so quick to overlook the sabotaged brakes? Was he involved somehow? What about the sheriff's department? Why weren't they taking the earlier threats against Gemma seriously?

From what Gray knew of Sheriff Kruse, he believed the sheriff was a good man. But he had too much square acreage to cover with a few deputies and even less funding. So Gray could give him some grace, but he didn't like what sounded like a well-developed routine of letting Gemma's neighbors get away with harassment with nothing more than a slap on the wrist and the hope that it would stop on its own.

Fury boiled up in Gray's gut. He crushed the soda can in his hand. When the time was right, Gray would talk to the sheriff but not yet. Not until he had the information he needed. Gemma didn't know just how fortuitous Gray's arrival was.

Will you listen to yourself?

He hadn't come here to help her. He'd come to

Tiger Mountain as a way to slip into the trafficking organization and work with them while garnering the information he'd required for arrests. He should be looking into the man Gemma had mentioned today—the investor, Clyde Morris, in addition to the other staff and volunteers.

After grabbing another can of soda, Gray sat at his laptop to work. It was going to be a long night. First, he sent off an email to Kit Howard, the forensic investigator, and detailed what he'd learned so far. He wanted to hear what Kit made of it. Could the vandalism Gemma equated to sabotage—that the sheriff's department didn't take seriously—be related to attempted murder via tampered brakes?

Then he started in on his research on Clyde Morris who headed up an organization called Conservation International. However, the sanctuary had been funded through another company, Investments Conglomerate. What a vague name. A shell company owned by Clyde Morris, perhaps? That's why Gray hadn't known about him. And that would make it easy to launder and traffic any kind of contraband. Wildlife trafficking and anonymous companies went hand in hand.

Mark was using his channels to pull additional information on Clyde and send it to Gray. He had his work cut out for him tonight. The man himself would show up tomorrow, and Gray needed to know everything he could. He wanted to either draw attention to himself in the right way or stay invisible and observe.

He started with the Tiger Mountain website. Immediately images of Gemma's tigers popped up. A few pictures of Gemma were in the photo gallery but always with the sunglasses, and that got Gray thinking about her eyes.

Those gorgeous eyes…

She was an amazing woman. But he wouldn't let that distract him. He had to keep his head clear to get justice for Bill. And if closing this case put him in a good position for the promotion that might finally earn his father's approval, then that would just be the proverbial buttercream icing on the red velvet cake.

The next day Gray found himself partnering with Wes—the intern working at the sanctuary for college credit this semester—to learn about the daily rigors of cleaning the habitats and feeding the tigers, just like Gemma had told him he would last night. She'd said it as though he might be surprised or unwilling to do the mundane and lowly work of shoveling muck, but he'd done enough volunteer work around animals to know the drill. He hadn't seen her today, but that was probably for the best. He had to stay focused.

He should get to know all the volunteers and

staff. Cara and Tom were full-time. Jill, Mavis and Ernie were volunteers like Gray and worked varied shifts. Gemma detailed the daily schedules and chores on a whiteboard in the kitchen slash conference room of the resource building where everyone gathered for their morning meetings, supplies throughout the day, and for weekly and monthly meetings. Every single thing they did for the tigers was written in task-specific binders. Meticulous, grueling work, as far as Gray could tell. But everyone he'd met seemed committed to the cause and loved the tigers. He could almost doubt the tip he'd received.

Then there was Clyde, whom Gray had yet to meet but according to Gemma would arrive today. Someone from the sheriff's office was also coming this morning to investigate the effigy doll and the tampered brakes. At least, he hoped Gemma would tell them about the brakes. He'd call in the information himself, but he didn't want to risk being recognized by Sheriff Kruse. But with his head down as he walked the habitat, tidying and picking up old bones, he was sure no one would notice him. This was perfect. He could watch the others like one of the cats stalking its prey. Gray's prey was suspicious activity.

Wes snuck up behind him in the grass. "I finished with Caesar's habitat. Once you're done here, we can finish the other two and then let the cats back out and clean their stalls. Then feed them. After this, we move on to the next habitat building. Need help here or you want to finish this one on your own?"

"I'm good. You go ahead and start on the next one."

Wes gestured toward the fence. "There's Deputy Callahan now, coming to check out Kayla's habitat."

Gemma walked next to the deputy, showing him where they'd discovered the effigy last night.

Great. Gray knew the deputy. He would definitely be recognized if he got too close and then what?

Gray kept his head down and headed into the taller grass to the other side, where he still needed to clean. For some reason, Wes followed him.

"Gemma mentioned some incidents, but she didn't share too much," Gray said. "What do you know about who is behind this?"

Wes shrugged. "We all think it's probably Emil Atkins—or that he's the ringleader, if it's a group of people. He claims that the sounds and scents of the tigers disturb his horses and cattle. He seems to think if he messes with Gemma enough she might get tired of it and leave. Or if he causes her some problems, she might have to shut the sanctuary down. We have our first official USDA inspection coming up and then, we'll get surprise inspections, you know."

Gray seriously wanted a reason to meet Mr. Atkins. Wes paused before heading up the trail to the gate. "I heard you were with her last night when you found the doll."

"Yep. It scared her, but she's a strong person and got over it pretty quickly."

"Maybe the deputy needs to talk to you too."

Great. All he needed was Wes butting into it. "I'm sure they know where to find me if they want me."

The intern nodded and then left Gray to his work. But he didn't trust Wes not to fetch the deputy. Gray slipped out of the habitat and headed in the opposite direction. He'd have to make up an excuse to give Wes later.

He made his way to the resource building, avoiding others. He didn't want anyone questioning his exit. After grabbing some water, he made small talk with Cara, so she'd pass the word on to Gemma that Gray would return later. He hoped Deputy Callahan would make short work of his investigation and leave.

But as he stepped out of the office, Gemma and Deputy Callahan entered through the main door. Gray froze. He whirled around to head out the back.

A man he didn't recognize stood in his way. "Everything all right?"

"Sure, yes. I just realized I forgot something up at the habitat where I was working." Yeah, he hadn't finished his task. "Just heading there now."

The man cocked a brow. The look in his eyes told Gray he didn't believe him.

Why?

Gray started to walk around, hearing Gemma and the deputy's conversation growing louder. Gemma sounded frustrated, her voice louder than he would have expected, and the deputy's tone seemed to brush off her accusations.

He wanted to turn around and face off with that man behind the badge. Give him a piece of his mind. Meanwhile this guy…this man who stood in his path had to be Clyde Morris, himself. Gray was not making a good first impression.

It was now or never. Gray thrust out his hand. "I don't believe we've met. I'm Gray Wilson."

Clyde's hand came up to meet Gray's, though slowly, hesitantly. "Clyde Morris."

"Mr. Morris, I still have some work to do. Care to walk with me?"

Clyde looked over Gray's shoulder, weighing his options. Something like disdain flashed in the man's gaze and then he looked at Gray. "Let's go for that walk. And please, call me Clyde."

Interesting. Clyde Morris didn't want a run-in with Deputy Callahan any more than Gray did, but he'd wager, for far different reasons. He pushed through the back exit and held the door for Clyde.

"I'm volunteering. Just started yesterday. How about you, Clyde? You a volunteer or a staffer? What do you do at Tiger Mountain?"

Clyde kept the brisk pace with Gray. "I'm the bread and butter here. I'm the man who funded the initiative to get this place going. Hopefully, Gemma will be able to gain the attention of wildlife philanthropists and raise more funds on her own."

"What about the reason Deputy Callahan is here? Got any ideas on what to do about this troublemaker, whoever he is?"

Clyde stopped walking so Gray stopped too. "Oh, I know who you are now. Gemma told me about you. You're the guy who was with her last night when she found that effigy."

"That's right. You don't think this Emil Atkins might actually try to harm her physically, do you?"

Clyde frowned. "Why so interested?"

Gray shrugged. "Why not? She seems like a nice lady. I don't want to see her get hurt."

Now, here was the rub. Should Gray ask Clyde about Gemma's brakes? He didn't want to give Clyde any reason to look at him too closely.

Maybe he should wait on that conversation. Might as well play dumb as long as he could.

To his surprise, Clyde clapped him on the back. "I don't either, Gray. I don't either. Gemma is like a daughter to me. At least now, anyway, that her family is gone. I funded this project of hers because years ago I was friends with her father and uncle. We shared a few business ventures, interests and wildlife conservation efforts, including the original sanctuary right on this same property. Then, we called it Tiger Hills. When Gemma's parents died, her uncle stepped in to care for her and keep their sanctuary going. But then he died, too. I was involved in a project on another continent and wasn't here to offer much help, financially or otherwise, during either tragedy. When she came to me with her idea to build a new sanctuary—with a new name and a fresh start—how could I say no?"

Gray studied the man. "I see your point."

"Bottom line is that I won't idly stand by while people threaten Gemma, nor will I allow her to get hurt. By you or anyone else. That's why I'm here—to investigate who's behind this harassment and stop it."

Funny that he didn't want to talk to the deputy. That should have been his natural response. It would have been Gray's too, if he weren't working undercover.

Clyde squeezed Gray's shoulder blade. Gray almost winced. What was that about? But the man had certainly got his attention. He looked him straight in the eye.

"Gemma has enough on her plate. If you see anything suspicious, anything at all, will you come to me first?"

What was he going to say? No? Nodding, Gray said, "I will."

Gray had already decided he needed to stick close to Gemma as much as possible, to keep her safe. Clyde's words had surprised him. Hadn't he come here to investigate crimes that might involve someone like this man who'd funded Tiger Mountain? And now, it turned out that Clyde was here at Tiger Mountain to conduct his own investigation.

Another twist in Gray's investigation.

FIVE

Gemma watched Clyde walk alongside Gray as they made their way into the sanctuary and habitats. She didn't know why it mattered, but she was glad to see them walking along like they were friends. She'd wanted Clyde to meet Gray. For some reason she couldn't fathom, she wanted him to like Gray too. She couldn't help but wonder if adding Gray or Clyde to this conversation with Deputy Callahan would make a difference. Without anyone there to be on her side, talking with the deputy clawed over her nerves.

Turning her attention back to Deputy Callahan, as they stood at his vehicle, she listened to his last words. "I'll write all this up in my report, Gemma, but there's not much I can do about it until we know who's behind it. We can only speculate and that's not good enough."

Like she hadn't heard those words a million times. "I'll see about getting some security cameras going. But it's just another expense to add to my wish list."

"If you want some real evidence we can use, better make those cameras a priority."

"I don't get it. It seems like I'm the one being punished here. I have to pay for security cameras to catch these guys while harassing me doesn't cost them a thing. You have an idea who is behind it. Why can't you just stop him?"

The way he snapped his small writing pad closed made it clear he hadn't liked her insinuation that he wasn't doing his job. He arched a brow. "Anything else you can think of, Gemma?"

She frowned. The sheriff's office heard from her often and now, with each new incident, she felt like her complaints were being relegated to a low priority. Discouraged, she sighed. The image of Gray walking with Clyde entered her mind. And then his words.

Tell them about the attempt on your life. Tell them about your brakes. Promise me?

She hadn't promised him because she hadn't wanted to, but now she found herself responding to his request. "Actually, there is something else."

If she expected the deputy to take her seriously, then there were things that Gemma needed to take seriously as well. Deputy Callahan's reaction would be interesting to see.

"Well?"

"I had a wreck yesterday on the county road that runs through the property."

"And you're just reporting it now? What happened?" Deputy Callahan flipped open his little notebook again, the sheriff's department funds too low to bring them into the millennium. Or perhaps Callahan preferred pen and paper. Gemma got that. She used a whiteboard.

"Someone tampered with my brakes."

His entire forehead creased as he raised his brows. "Say again?"

"My brakes. I think someone tampered with them so I wouldn't be able to stop and I'd go over the edge."

"Are you saying someone tried to kill you?"

"Yes."

"And you know this how?"

"One of my new volunteers helped Tom tow the CJ over to Carl's. He checked out the Jeep when they arrived."

"And what did Carl say?"

Oh, why had she brought it up? She should have talked to Carl first, but Gray said the mechanic only gave the brakes a passing glance.

"I'm going to have Carl look at it again. I don't think he looked it over very carefully."

The deputy wrote some more in his notepad. Then he flipped it closed, concern in his eyes. That surprised Gemma.

"I'll stop by and talk to the mechanic myself." The deputy put his hands on his hips and gave her a pointed look. "Why would someone want to kill you, Gemma?"

"I don't…I don't know. You don't think it's just whoever has been harassing the sanctuary hoping I would shut things down and leave, do you?"

He shook his head. "Everything else so far has just been pranks. I don't think this prankster is the murdering type. The harassing type, yes, but I don't think he would kill someone. That said, you've made some people pretty angry with what you've decided to do here. Maybe you should have considered the neighbors when you decided to start this thing up again. Sure, it's a new name and new management but it's the same old thing. You should have thought about the trouble your parents had here, your uncle too, before they died."

His words cut through her. She didn't know what to make of them.

"Still, let me talk to the sheriff about this. I think it's high time we crack down on the harassment against you, and I know you want it to stop. It's taking up too much of my time and I want it stopped, too." Something flashed in Callahan's eyes, too quickly for her to read, before he stared at the ground. Then when he looked back up to her, the emotion was gone. "In the meantime, you'd better keep an eye out. Beware of strangers."

"What about…what about people I know?"

"Say again?"

"I'm just thinking that maybe it wasn't a stranger who tampered with my brakes. Maybe it was someone I know."

"And I'll ask again, any reason someone you know would want to kill you? Make it look like an accident?"

She shook her head.

Thoughts of her parents' plane crash rattled through her along with images of the wreck that killed her uncle, crushing her chest so she couldn't breathe.

"Gemma, you okay?"

She drew in a breath, composed herself. "Yes, I'm fine. How's…how's Sandy? I'm sorry I didn't ask you right off." Through all of this she'd discovered that his wife was fighting cancer, but she hadn't learned more than that.

His expression turned grim. "Hanging in there. Thank you for asking." He hung his head. Then when he glanced back up to Gemma, more feelings that she couldn't decipher briefly appeared in his eyes. "I'm sorry you're going through this, Gemma."

"I wish I knew something more to tell you."

He nodded and started to get into his vehicle.

"Um… Deputy Callahan?"

"Yes?" He paused, halfway into the vehicle.

"The night my uncle was killed, he was about to tell me something. I have always had the feeling it was something big. I've wondered if maybe someone had wanted him dead and somehow caused the wreck. Do you think that's possible?"

"You were how old then? Seventeen?"

"I'd just turned eighteen."

"It was a traumatic event, and you were at that age when everything seems like it's life-or-death important. Maybe you imagined the importance of what he planned to tell you. Blew things out of proportion. I wouldn't make too much of it. The crash was ruled an accident. Remember, hon, it was a rainy night and a treacherous road."

He pursed his lips and studied her, like he was concerned about her mental state, which might plant doubts in his mind about everything Gemma had said. She wished now she hadn't brought it up.

"Get some rest, Gemma. Take a few days off." He climbed into his vehicle and drove off.

Right, like she could take time off when she had so much to do. She was almost certain not all of the habitats had been cleaned today, and they still had to butcher a slab of beef to feed the tigers this evening. And chickens for Caesar. He only liked chicken. Tomorrow the vet was coming to check on the old tiger. He might have liver cancer.

Gemma rubbed her arms and searched the woods that surrounded the sanctuary. The Wild Rogue Wilderness, where Gray said he'd been when he'd heard her shouting for help.

Movement drew her gaze to the carport shadows next to the main building.

Wes was talking to Emil Atkins! What was Emil even doing here? What was Wes doing *with* him?

He'd better be telling the man to get lost.

Gemma wished Deputy Callahan had stayed a few minutes longer.

She squeezed her cane until her knuckles were white. Her heartbeat thudding through her, she marched toward the building. When the two men disappeared behind the wall, she rushed forward, her leg aching with the effort, and called out. By the time she made the side of the building, both men had disappeared.

Fury coursed through her. Could Wes be involved with Emil? Was this the connection? Had he been the one to leave the effigy in Kayla's habitat?

Clyde had taken a phone call, leaving Gray free to finish cleaning the habitat while thinking about their strange conversation. He wished he could have lingered to listen in on the call. Clyde wasn't the man that Gray had expected. That's what he got for bringing his presumptions with him. He'd assumed the man was guilty based on limited information, but Clyde came across as innocent and genuinely concerned about Gemma. Still, Gray knew better than to trust Clyde. After all these years, if he were heading up the ring, the man had to be practiced in living his persona as an upstanding citizen. Someone fighting for the conservation of endangered tigers.

A true sanctuary stood in direct contrast to trafficking by rescuing abused or neglected animals, providing care. A true sanctuary didn't commercialize the tigers. Didn't buy, sell or trade the animals except where necessary for the tiger's quality of life.

Those thoughts brought him back to the task. He had a responsibility here in addition to his investigation.

The big cats were still in their stalls and off their schedule. He searched for Wes, but the guy was nowhere to be found. Gray didn't want to tackle the stalls without knowing the exact mechanism and procedure for releasing the tigers outside and locking them out of the stalls. He could probably figure it out on his own, but if he got it wrong that situation could turn dangerous. Even deadly.

Still, the work needed to be done. Where was Wes? He could ask one of the others to show him, but he had a feeling Wes wouldn't appreciate it. He didn't want to make enemies.

Frowning, Gray instead went in search of Gemma. He wanted to find out about her conversation with the deputy and keep an eye on her in general. She hadn't asked Gray to protect her, and he had no reason to be too worried for her safety in the middle of the day with the volunteers and staff about, except Gray couldn't find her anywhere.

Inside the resource building, Gray headed to the office and spotted Cara through the window walking to her parked car. It was only midafternoon—where was she going? Gray followed her outside.

"Cara!" He picked up his pace to catch her.

She paused next to her Honda Civic. "What's up?"

"Have you seen Gemma?"

"She was with the deputy, but I haven't seen her since." She frowned. "Why?"

He shrugged. "I wanted to talk to her, and I can't find her."

"I'm sure she's around somewhere. I know she wanted to check on Kayla after Deputy Callahan left. Maybe check the habitat."

"Sure thing." But he had just been there and no Gemma.

Cara got in her car and drove away. Gray stood there and scanned the woods. From here he couldn't see much of the sanctuary behind the trees. Off in the distance, he spotted movement on a trail.

Gemma?

Per his mission, he needed to make inroads with Gemma and, now, Clyde. And he had a good excuse to talk to her. He could ask how it went with the deputy. Plus, he'd come up with an idea for educating the public. She didn't have to know the specifics about his years of experience in the wildlife arena. He trailed after her hoping to catch up with her. This particular path hedged the sanctuary expansion program—a vision to bring in more big cats and perhaps one day add other abused wildlife. It had beautiful views overlooking the Wild Rogue Wilderness region—rugged gorges and old-growth forests. The deeper into the forest on the trail, the thicker and taller the oaks, madrone, tan oak and chinquapin trees grew...the darker the forest.

Was she hiking the trail, which couldn't be easy with her cane, because she needed some time to herself?

Gray reconsidered interrupting her, but decided that he would follow behind, just to watch out for her. It didn't seem to him that Gemma was all that concerned about her life. Had she forgotten someone had tampered with her brakes? Didn't she understand what a bloodied effigy meant?

Did she realize that even Clyde appeared concerned for her? Though, come to think of it, could the man's concern for Gemma be an act?

Hands in his pockets, Gray hiked the trail, staying back to give Gemma the space she needed. And he thought about Clyde.

Could the man be behind the trafficking, using Tiger Mountain, and yet still care about Gemma as if she was a daughter? To Gray's way of thinking, those two undertakings were diametrically opposed. Gemma loved the sanctuary and the cats; any attempt to harm them would be painful to her. Things weren't adding up. As he walked, the trees closed in and the trail narrowed, littered with rocks and pebbles and gnarled tree roots. Hard for a woman with a cane, but Gemma had it figured out. And Gray thought he might have her figured out. She must doubt his assessment of the brakes or that someone had tampered with them. That someone was trying to kill her. She wasn't taking this seriously. Either that or it was simply too difficult for her to imagine someone harming her in broad daylight.

The woods around him suddenly turned quiet as the birdsong and chatter of squirrels and forest animals stilled. Leaves shuddered with a breeze. The sense that someone watched them set his teeth on edge.

His years in law enforcement, on top of his experience in the forests, sent warning signals resounding through him. The trail twisted around a cliffside, switching back above him. Pebbles trickled and Gray looked straight up the rocky wall. Was someone up there?

Gemma could be in danger.

He refocused on the trail and Gemma stood there, glaring at him.

"What are you doing here, Gray? Are you following me?"

"You got me. I followed you." He didn't mean to grin, exactly, because he wanted to remind her she shouldn't be hiking alone, but she somehow made him smile. Her long brown hair glistened in a ray of sun that broke through the trees. Beautiful. Gray found it hard to concentrate. He had the sudden urge to run his fingers through the tendrils. He shifted his gaze to her eyes and caught his mistake too late. Her eyes would always be a distraction for him.

To his surprise, Gemma's face softened. "You did?" Her question was soft. Warm even.

"Yes," Gray said, his voice softer too. *What are you doing, man? You can't be flirting with this woman!* But her eyes stared back at him, so full of goodness and purpose and worry all tangled up together. "You shouldn't go places alone. Remember, someone tried to kill you."

"I've walked this trail a hundred times."

"That was before someone tampered with your brakes."

Gemma sagged a little. "Oh, that. I wish you would quit reminding me. I needed to think about something else."

But he could see it in her eyes—even if she wasn't thinking about the brakes, she was brooding over something else that bothered her. How had he become so in tune with Gemma Rollins? "What happened, Gemma?"

She leaned harder on her cane, propped between two rocks. "Nothing. I wanted to clear my thoughts. I don't know who I can trust anymore."

"What did the deputy say? You did tell him about the brakes, didn't you?"

She nodded. "He said he would talk to Carl and see what he thinks. You said Carl gave it a cursory glance. Do you think he'll look again and find the same thing you saw? Or did I just make a fool of myself in front of a deputy who already doesn't take me seriously? Sometimes I even wonder if he wants the sanctuary gone, too."

Gemma leaned on the cane with both hands now and it was all Gray could do not to rush to her and hold her up. But she was much too independent to accept that from him. He didn't doubt she could hold her own, either. It was just that... maybe she had never had to face this kind of pressure from all sides.

He didn't want to give up his cover. Not yet. "I don't want to think Carl's involved, but if he doesn't tell the deputy the truth, then we'll know at least one person involved in this."

She shook her head. "I've known him much too long. I would never believe that."

And that was Gemma's problem. "You trust too much, Gemma." Gray stepped closer. He could catch her if she fell, but not for one minute did he believe she would.

"I think you're right," she replied. "I trust people I don't even know. Like you. I trust you when I shouldn't. I don't even know you."

How could he make her understand he was here to help her? But that wasn't true either. What was he thinking? Helping Gemma Rollins had never been part of his mission parameters. He was here to finish this, to find the person who was not only responsible for Bill's death but also the head of a large wildlife trafficking ring.

What would he do if that person turned out to be Clyde Morris, the man whom Gemma considered a father figure? From the information he'd read on Clyde, the man had long been a part of the Rollins family clan, though he hadn't been much support for Gemma when her parents and then her uncle were killed.

"Listen, Gemma, I'm sorry about the deputy. And about everything that's happening. But I do have some good news. I came up with an idea for educating the public. I wanted to tell you about that when I saw you on the trail. Then I realized that maybe you wanted some privacy so I tried to give you that while following you to make sure you were all right."

Her eyes brightened. "You came up with an idea for me? What—"

A rumble above cut off her question. Rocks shifted above, crashed against the cliffside and echoed across the mountain and through the trees.

"Look out!" Gray grabbed Gemma, cane and all, and pressed her beneath a protruding part of the rock wall, covering her with his body. Protecting her. Her breaths came hard and fast against his neck as her fear mingled with his own.

God, please protect her. Protect us!

SIX

The roar of boulders, rocks and dirt falling resounded through her ears and rumbled through her core. The rock wall behind her shook as if the whole earth quaked.

Gray's weight pressed against her as he pushed her harder against the granite. He was covering her, protecting her—making sure she didn't get hurt. This was a matter of life and death, after all. Gemma tried to shove the panic down, but a cry escaped anyway, betraying her. She squeezed her eyes shut as though that would help her keep the danger at bay, but whimpering groans fought their way out.

The rockslide seemed to take an eternity.

Gemma had never been more terrified, except in the crash with her uncle. What was happening to her already tumultuous life?

Finally, quiet replaced the roar in her ears. Well, quiet and her gulps for air along with Gray's.

Gray whispered into her ear, his warm breath accompanying his words. "I hope I didn't hurt you."

The fear and panic drained away, taking all her energy with it. Gemma was certain she would collapse if it weren't for the rock-hard pillar holding her up—and the powerfully built man. This wasn't the first time she'd felt the strength in Gray's shoulders and the sculpted muscles in his chest and abdomen. She'd been more than aware of his physique when he'd briefly carried her. She had to distract herself.

"Is it over?" she asked in a whisper.

"I think so." Gray slowly moved away from her. "Did I hurt you?" His tenderness was nearly her undoing. What did he think? That she would blame him for the pain she endured while being pressed against the rocks? He'd saved her life. Again. "No. I'm okay."

Did he suspect her lie? So what if the rock wall had likely left a few bruises on her back? At least she and Gray were still alive. Before stepping away from the wall, Gray twisted his neck to look behind him. They were partially pinned in by the rockslide. The way he tensed, she could practically feel the anger surging through him.

With all the rain they'd gotten, the rocks had no doubt shifted easily from their centuries-long resting place. A rockslide wasn't all that improbable, but what were the chances one would happen at the exact moment Gemma and Gray stood at that spot on the trail? Especially in light of her near death experience yesterday.

"Are you going to take this seriously now?"

Gemma couldn't help her quick intake of breath. The man didn't mince words. His question told her he had been thinking the same thing. This was no accident. "You don't think someone did this on purpose, do you?" The question sounded silly. But Gemma held on to a sliver of hope.

"We have to consider that a strong possibility." Gray turned to her, their faces impossibly close. "Gemma, why would someone want to kill you?"

"I don't know. All I can think is they don't want the sanctuary here. But is that worth ending my life?"

"The reasons people kill rarely make sense. Nothing is worth a person's life. Still, I want you to think hard about this. If you died, who would be left to run the sanctuary? Or would it die with you?"

At his words, a shudder ran over her. He didn't sound like a contract programmer who volunteered at a wildlife sanctuary in his free time. He sounded like someone who dealt with life-or-death issues every day.

Clearly sensing that she needed a minute to think through her response, he stepped away and assisted her around the large heap of rocks and dirt that must weigh a ton or more. They could have been crushed where they stood. Gray watched the area, alert and aware of his surroundings, to make sure they were no longer being threatened, she presumed. In a way, he reminded her of the tigers, always watching and patrolling their habitats, maintaining control of their territories. But that didn't boost her confidence in this predicament.

Would Gemma survive this?

Did she have the fortitude to stay and champion the sanctuary for the tigers' sake even when it could cost her life? "I'm the one with the vision. It's my dream. But Clyde was behind this too, and he wants the sanctuary. He could keep it going if something happened." *This time...* But she kept those words to herself.

She didn't know why he hadn't stepped in before. Maybe things were too far gone by the time he'd received the news. Or maybe he hadn't had the time or money and was too far away. She didn't know and she hadn't asked.

He'd only been a silent partner to begin with.

By the time she'd emerged from the hospital, her body, heart and mind broken, it had been much too late. She hadn't looked back because it was too painful so moved forward with her life.

But her heart always went back to wanting to

provide a home for endangered animals. Big cats. So after school, she'd gone to him with her idea to start a new sanctuary and had been more than relieved with his excitement at her idea. For the first time in a very long time, Gemma had been happy.

Still, she wished she hadn't answered Gray's question, said the words out loud, as though saying them would seal her fate, somehow. And now, her wounded leg ached more than ever, pain brought on by the strain of the hike and the stress of the rockslide. Gray handed over her cane as though sensing her suffering. He'd protected it? Kept it intact in the face of a rockslide? She looked up into his warm, brown eyes. "Thank you."

He nodded. "You're welcome."

Something unexpected—forbidden even— passed between them. Gemma couldn't say what. Oh, that wasn't true. She knew exactly what it was—an attraction, both physical and spiritual. A deep, emotional need for one another. She turned from him. She wouldn't let him see the answering response in her gaze. She couldn't trust him like that. Somehow, she had to recover her resolve. People hid who they really were. Gray had shown up yesterday and look how far he'd maneuvered himself into her life. The way he made her feel took her back to Ellis, the intern who had come to help at the sanctuary when her uncle was alive and running things. Gemma had been young and naive and let herself fall for him in a big way. He'd seemed to return her affections. She would have given him everything. Gone anywhere and done anything with him. Perhaps he would have taken advantage of that, if he'd had more time— but then his fiancée showed up at the sanctuary. He'd kept the news that he was engaged to himself until that moment. And then Ellis had the nerve to beg Gemma not to say anything about their relationship. It would ruin his life with the woman he really loved. If Gemma loved him, he'd said, then she would want him to be happy.

A rock shifted in the pile, jolting her back to the present. Gray studied her.

Using her cane and ignoring her trembling leg, she stepped away from him and just kept going. She needed to get down to the buildings, to her friends, both the staff and volunteers. People she knew. Gray might have saved her twice now, but who was he really? Strange that supposed attempts on her life all started happening when he showed up.

He, too, was hiding something, just like they all had been doing. Her parents, her uncle. Ellis, whom she'd fallen in love with when she was too young to know better. But she was much older, much wiser now.

"Hey, wait up."

Gemma kept walking. Though Gray had protected her and assisted her around the pile of boulders that now blocked her favorite trail, Gemma needed air and space. A small part of her knew she was hurting him by rejecting his help. But she didn't know him. Suspicion and paranoia whirled inside, easily invading her thoughts.

"Gemma, don't go alone. Please, don't ever be alone again until we find out who is behind this. Stick close to someone you trust, if not me."

Gray wasn't far behind her, fulfilling his self-proclaimed role as protector, but at least he was giving her the option to choose.

Clyde was the only man she could trust. She'd known him for years. She had to find out if he knew who might try to kill her and why. Then there was the matter of Wes. Clyde had added Wes—an intern from Oregon State University— to the staff two months ago himself. But how well did Clyde know him? She hadn't even thought to question that decision. Wes had been assigned a cabin on the far side of the facilities, but, as far as she knew, he hadn't stayed there even one night. But he had family close by so why would he?

Why had he been talking to Emil in the shadows? A secret rendezvous right here at the sanctuary? Bile rose in her throat. She'd have to confront Wes. She'd talk to Clyde about him first, though.

Given her strange sense of déjà vu, Gemma couldn't help but think the problems from the past and the issues in the present were somehow connected.

In that case, she didn't hold out much hope that she would live through this.

A week later, Gray was no closer to discovering anything at Tiger Mountain that could help him with his trafficking investigation. He was developing relationships with the Tiger Mountain staff that could prove invaluable. But he had the sense that time was not on his side.

More intel had been gathered from other agencies regarding Clyde Morris, revealing his shell companies. Kit had replied to Gray's email and asked for additional information. Based on the limited details Gray had shared, he suggested that vandalism, even in the form of an effigy, was not usually committed by someone willing to commit murder. He left it open for Gray to send additional information as he acquired it. That news hadn't surprised Gray, but at the same time left him baffled.

Maybe the cameras would solve the puzzle.

Gray had installed security cameras after convincing Clyde to pay for them. Cameras could have long ago solved the vandalism problem.

Why had it been so difficult to get the budget for them?

Except the cameras hadn't caught a thing three nights ago when someone had gotten into the sanctuary and freed a white tiger name Callie. Mavis and Ernie had been the ones to discover her. Thankfully, they were able to lure her back into her habitat with food instead of having to resort to a tranquilizer gun. Neither of them had been hurt, but it could have been a deadly encounter.

The cameras had caught their actions, but not the person responsible.

So Gray conducted surveillance at night, which reminded him of his game-warden days when he'd hidden, camouflaged by nature, and waited on poachers—those illegally fishing and hunting. If the poachers could use darkness as a cover, then so could Gray and it's what had made him a successful game warden, moving up the ranks quickly. Not that that had ever seemed to matter to his father.

Tonight, he'd found the perfect spot between two boulders wedged a quarter of the way up the mountain overlooking Tiger Mountain's buildings and habitats. Of course, he couldn't see the entire property, but any nefarious activity would probably happen near the facilities.

Though it was spring, the night was cold, dropping to the forties. With his black jacket and cap, Gray melted into the darkness. Pulling out his Dark Strider night vision binoculars, he settled in for the evening. He'd catch a few hours of sleep in the morning before he was on for his volunteer shift.

He reminded himself that he hadn't come to the sanctuary to help Gemma learn who left effigies and otherwise tormented her and the big cats or to find who was trying to kill her. But, on the other hand, it wasn't unusual for the parameters of a mission to expand or change. From his perch, he could also keep an eye on her cabin. Nobody would be able to approach without Gray noticing.

Ever since the rockslide, Gemma had kept her distance from him. His fault. He'd moved in a little too fast. At first Gemma had seemed to trust easily, but now he was hard pressed to earn her trust, especially since the attacks against her had escalated since Gray had arrived. Gray could tell that when she trusted people, she did so without reservation. Loved deeply without condition. And yet she remained somewhat wary of him. He didn't like it, even though he knew she had good reason to be on her guard.

Still, he found himself wanting her to trust him.

He'd never forget that moment, right after the rockslide, when she'd looked at him with suspicion. A twinge of hurt had pinched him, surprising him. He blamed himself for letting her get under his skin so quickly. Maybe it had to do with the life-or-death situations they had been through together and her eyes. He couldn't stop thinking about her eyes.

But he had to stop because, even now, thinking about her eyes was pulling his attention away from his mission. All he had to do was catch the person responsible for killing Bill, slaughtering tigers and selling their parts, other horrendous crimes against wildlife and much more.

Right now, Clyde was his top suspect. He had the wherewithal to be part of a wildlife trafficking ring. And with his global enterprises he definitely had the connections.

This wouldn't be the first time this same property, operating as a sanctuary, was under suspicion. Whether rumors or actual abuse, the sanctuary had lost funding and Clyde had been conveniently absent when everything fell apart. Gray wasn't sure what Clyde's real connection with the previous sanctuary had been, but he did know in his gut that he was going to nail this guy. He had to, for Bill. It didn't hurt that Gray was up for the promotion and bringing down the head of this trafficking ring would carry a lot of weight.

A raccoon skittered by him, paused and looked at Gray. Chattering, it scrambled away.

He hoped someone would make a move tonight. That way he could expose the person vandalizing the sanctuary and possibly the person or persons trying to kill Gemma.

Gemma, Gemma. He couldn't solve this soon enough. He needed to get away from her. He was all about protecting the innocent—the wildlife—but after he was done protecting Gemma, stopping her stalker, he had to protect his heart from her. Trying for love never ended well for him.

He'd walked around with a chip on his shoulder as a kid. He'd resented Cooper, because their father paid his older brother all the attention. Gray thought back to when he was twelve years old. He'd worked for two months on a homemade bow and arrow for his father. Built it himself, and all he could think about was that look in his father's eyes. He'd seen him give Coop the look. Gray had wanted that too. He'd given the bow and arrow to his father, only to have Cooper rush in and steal all the attention away with an announcement of some award he'd won. His father had put Gray's gift on the table without a second glance and given Cooper that look.

Gray had grabbed the present, run out the door and thrown it in the trash outside. That day, he stopped expecting anything from his father—his approval or attention—and resolved that he would forge his own way and never again need anyone.

But Gray hadn't realized just how messed up he'd been over the way his father treated him until he finally fell in love in his midtwenties. Yeah, it had taken him that long to find what he'd thought was the right woman. And then… Gray ruined it all by expecting something from her. Approval, validation? He wasn't sure. But when he showed up at her door with a ring—a diamond solitaire engagement ring—and saw her kissing another guy through the front window, he went right back to that day with his dad. It was the same thing all over again. Him counting on someone else to love him and make him feel valued.

Never again. He'd said the words before, and he wouldn't be fooled twice. Now? He made it his job to protect the innocent—the animals and endangered species—while always keeping his distance emotionally. Trying to get closer to another person would only lead to disaster.

One of the tigers growled and roared, yanking Gray back to the moment.

Gray shifted, moving his night vision binoculars to the habitats. Had he missed something? Or was the sound just a—there it was again. No. That was definitely a growl. The big cat was in defensive mode.

Gray wanted to go and investigate, but he could see more if he stayed where he was and watched. Otherwise, he might miss the culprit, if someone was there causing trouble for Gemma by messing with her big cats. Fury stirred in Gray's stomach. This was the moment he'd been out here waiting for, night after night. Still...

The vandalism had to stop! He started to climb down so he could catch them in the act.

In the distance to his left, he heard the distinctive sound of a door shutting. He whirled and turned his binoculars to the cabin, spotting Gemma as she exited.

Oh, no! *Gemma, what are you doing?*

That was it. Gray scrambled from his perch between the boulders to head her off. With everything that had happened, she didn't need to walk the grounds alone.

He hadn't felt the buzz of his cell phone. Why hadn't she called him? At the very least, he'd thought she'd understood he would be there to protect her.

He pushed the disappointment aside. She didn't trust him, that's why. Gray wanted to call out to her, but he was too far away and he might alert whoever was at the habitat stirring up trouble. Gray couldn't be certain someone was there, but the cat's angry growls continued.

What's more, the way Gemma marched, even with her cane—that determined set of her chin and shoulders—said that she wasn't thinking past her anger and frustration to her own safety. He slid down a boulder and vaulted around a huge, thick cedar with gnarly roots until, finally, his boots hit flat ground. Gray took off after Gemma.

"Gemma," he called softly. "Wait for me."

He wasn't sure how he was going to explain his sudden appearance, but her safety was more important. Still she was too far ahead of him, and she quickly disappeared in the shadows. He heard the telltale sound of the gate opening and shutting. Saw the beam of her flashlight as she walked the paths within the main habitat settings. She would be looking for the troubled tiger and would find the problem and could expect—what? Another effigy?

Or could this lead to her death this time? Could the same person who had tampered with her brakes to kill her also be the person who was sabotaging the sanctuary? It seemed unlikely. Kit suggested otherwise, and even the sheriff's department considered the vandalism a simple matter of pranks.

Through the woods, in the distance, he spotted headlights from a vehicle driving up the road that led to the sanctuary. At the main gate, Gray slipped inside and shut the gate behind him before searching for the beam of light from Gemma's flashlight.

"Gemma!" he called out this time. He didn't care if he scared off the person behind the sabotage. In fact, he hoped they would be long gone by now. He didn't want to see Gemma hurt.

Taking the path, he rounded the corner of one of the large habitats. "Gemma!"

"Don't move." Her voice was low and measured.

He immediately stopped, heeding the warning in her tone. A question formed on his lips, but he never spoke the words. He didn't have to ask. He could see perfectly well the tiger standing in his path, tail swishing.

SEVEN

Gray remained frozen, his blood draining from his brain and heart into his feet. He couldn't move if he wanted to.

He'd experienced many things as a game warden and in his position as a USFWS special agent, but never had he faced off with a seven hundred pound cat. Never stared into a set of menacing tiger eyes without a protective barrier.

The animal he recognized as Raja studied him, moving his tail.

Swish, swish.

Swish, swish.

Gray thought he could see Raja trying to decide if Gray was prey—that is, dinner—or if he was a predator and a threat to Raja's territory. Either conclusion did not bode well for the outcome of this encounter. Gray considered his best course of action, the options playing through his mind all at once. He shoved aside any thoughts of his own safety—the natural fight-or-flight human response and survival instinct—and focused on Gemma. His Glock was shoved in a holster to his side, hidden away. It wouldn't do for Gemma to see that. He'd have even more explaining to do. But he'd use it, if necessary, to protect her life.

Eyes wide, she had her hands out, palms down, as though the action would keep everyone calm, including the tiger. "Raja, let's go back to where you're safe. Where you have food and water," she spoke softly to the beast.

To Gray, she said, "I raised Raja from a cub. He was only six months old when the owners lost their home and had to move into an apartment. A tiger cub wasn't something they could care for. He was our first cat here at the sanctuary and is two years old now."

Raja started chuffing—the sound tigers made instead of purring. Gray understood this to be a happy sound. Maybe Raja had lost interest in Gray. The tension in his shoulders eased but not too much.

Slowly dropping her hands, Gemma appeared to relax. "Raja…" She dragged his name out in a sing-song fashion.

Raja moved toward her and rubbed his head against her legs and waist and continued chuffing. Gemma patted his side like the big cat was a friendly Labrador retriever. She rubbed his head and played with his ears. "Are you a good boy, Raja?"

Yeah. Labrador retriever.

Sierra, the tiger in the habitat nearest them, paced along the fence. Next to her, Layla and Lilly, sister tigers who lived in the same habitat, paced as well. Gray hoped the beasts didn't growl or cause Raja to hurt Gemma. One could never forget that a tiger—no matter how it was raised—was a wild animal. A deadly wild animal. Raja clearly loved and responded to Gemma, but Gray knew things could turn dangerous in an instant. Raja could simply play with Gemma and then hurt her. Kill her. It happened all too often— trainers playing with tigers like they were small kitty cats and then the tiger attacked. Zookeepers and workers simply doing their jobs.

Be careful, Gemma...

Gray wanted to speak, to urge Gemma to be cautious and not careless. But she was the expert, and knew what she was doing, not him. He was more than nervous this close to a tiger. He also wanted to ask the best way to lure Raja into his habitat. What they needed was someone else to help. Someone who could either get at the tranquilizer gun or offer food to entice the tiger.

A sudden gush of water from a large hose blasted Raja in the face. A man held the hose, spraying the tiger. If Raja had been attacking

Gemma, then this might have been enough to free Gemma from the tiger's attack. But, instead, the tiger, who had been calm and playful a moment before, roared and slashed his paws through the air. Gray looked on in shock as Gemma was thrown back, her body landing on the concrete, head slamming against it. She didn't move.

"Nooooo!" Gray rushed forward to Gemma as the rush of water forced the tiger to retreat to the fence.

He lifted Gemma in his arms, searching for injuries. He saw no claw marks or blood, and her pulse was strong, but she didn't stir.

"What are you doing?" he yelled at the man. He recognized Wes. He must have been in the approaching vehicle.

Wes might have thought he was helping the situation, but the tiger was angry and frightened. And with no one else there to help lure the big cat away, someone was going to die if Gray didn't do something and fast.

"Keep the water on him. I'll get the dart gun."

Lifting Gemma, he carried her limp form as he rushed to the emergency lockbox, which was much too far away for comfort. He laid her down next to the box. She groaned. Good, she was waking up. Gray wanted nothing more than to hold her and reassure her. Comfort her. But he had no time.

It hit him that the lockbox was called a lock-box for a reason. "The key—I don't have a key." Gemma stared at him, confusion in her eyes. "Please, do you have keys to the lockbox?" *Come on, Gemma, snap out of it. I need your help here.*

Gray didn't want to have to put the big cat down with his Glock. Gemma would never forgive him. That bothered him more than he would have liked—a fact he found both confusing and surprising.

He started searching her for keys before she could react. "I'm sorry. I have to find the keys."

He found them attached to her belt loop. Gemma finally shook off her stupor, helping him.

"This one," she said.

His momentary relief faded when he heard the spray of water turn to a drizzle and then nothing at all. Had Wes somehow forced Raja into his habitat and locked the gate?

In answer to his question, the roar of an angry tiger on the loose filled the quiet sanctuary.

Gemma pressed her hand against the knot at the back of her head, but her thoughts were on Raja. Gray inserted darts into the gun.

"Let me do it. I'm trained in this. I don't want you hurting Raja." She sat up.

"How's your vision? Seeing double?"

Gemma frowned. Gray helped her up as dizziness swept over her. "I don't know."

Gray frowned. "Under the circumstances, I think I'm the one to do it."

Still, Gemma reached for the gun.

He held it just out of her reach but caught her as she stumbled. "Trust me, Gemma. I won't hurt Raja. It pains me to see him going through this too."

Gazing into Gray's eyes, she saw the truth of it there. He really did care about the big cats. He cared about her too, though she couldn't fathom why. And even stranger, Gemma felt herself drawn to this man she barely knew.

"I'm sorry that I wasn't able to grab your cane too. I'm sure it's still there somewhere. But I had to get you to safety."

"Thanks for that," she said, though she was still considering her response to his request to trust him.

Gray grabbed her arm and pulled her behind him. "Let's get this situation contained before anyone, including Raja, gets hurt."

"I don't understand what happened. How did Raja get out of his habitat?"

Gray paused and they both listened for sounds of the tiger or of Wes. "I think we both know the answer to that," he said.

Gemma hadn't wanted to admit that this could

be the work of the saboteurs again, but neither did she wish for the other possibilities—that a volunteer or staff worker had been negligent and left a habitat open. "If that's true, then this is going too far. Two tigers released in a week. The saboteur has never done anything like this before."

"You said saboteur this time. Singular. You mean Emil, don't you? You really think an old rancher is doing this, putting himself and his animals at risk?" Doubt suffused Gray's tone.

In the distance, Raja roared and growled his displeasure. He was confused, perhaps looking for a way to escape the sanctuary completely. *God, please no.* That would be disastrous. She could lose her license and funding completely. And Raja could lose his life outside of these walls. Bad enough he'd escaped into the sanctuary at large. "I hope Wes has found a safe place to hide."

"I'm not sure what happened. Did he purposefully turn the water off and if so, why?" Gray asked.

Gemma followed him, limping as she went. He headed toward Raja's bellows, cautiously watching the environment. She wasn't sure why she was letting him take the lead, but he projected so much confidence, while she still hadn't gained solid footing and wouldn't until she had her cane once again. No, that wasn't true. Even then, she would likely let him lead. Her brain still felt scrambled, and her limbs shook from the unexpected encounter with Raja. She was grateful that Raja had been the one to escape and not one of the more aggressive tigers like Zeus. He'd been terribly abused and didn't like or trust any of them. At least, not yet.

As her thoughts grew clear, something niggling at the recesses of her mind came into focus. "What was Wes doing here, Gray?"

"I saw a car approaching as I ran to the sanctuary. I think that might have been him, but I don't know. We'll ask when we find him. But he has a cabin in the back, doesn't he?"

"Yeah, we offered it to him, but he doesn't use it. His family lives nearby."

"That's what I thought."

"But, then, why were you here? What were you doing here?"

Gray turned to her then and she regretted her insinuation.

"I didn't let Raja out of his habitat, if that's what you mean."

"Then why? You weren't following me again, were you?"

His chest deflated with his breath. "Can we talk about this later? I had a good reason for being here."

Gemma knew she shouldn't trust a stranger,

but something about Gray compelled her to follow him now in her sanctuary to dart her tiger and to trust that he had good reasons. Was she losing her mind? Wes suddenly appeared behind them.

Gray stopped. "Where'd you come from?"

He pointed. "Over there. I was hiding from Raja."

"What were you doing here?" Gemma and Gray asked simultaneously.

Wes stepped back and held his hands up as though protecting himself from invisible darts. "I lost my cell phone and came to search for it in case I dropped it here. I knocked on your door, Gemma. With everything going on, I wanted you to know why I was in the sanctuary at night. Then I saw the flashlight beam in the sanctuary and came to investigate. Since you weren't home I thought you might be here and could help me find my cell."

"You could have called first," Gray said.

"Um…not without the numbers on my cell."

Good point. Gemma wanted to believe him, but she'd seen the man with Emil. She'd questioned him about it earlier, but he claimed he'd simply confronted the neighbor and reported the incident to Cara. Gemma didn't want to work with people whom she couldn't trust, but letting an intern go based on suspicions wasn't right either. She'd suffered from the suspicions of others with the rumors about her parents' sanctuary. She wouldn't stoop to dismiss someone based on circumstantial evidence. Still, she'd tried to keep an eye on him. And here he was in the middle of suspicious activity.

Just like Gray.

And then Raja lumbered through the grass next to the path. *Poor Raja!* Gray lifted the dart gun. "Take cover. Raja could run when he's hit. I don't want you to be in his path."

"Hand it over, Gray." Gemma held out her hand. "I know what I'm doing. You're not officially trained. Technical training is crucial. If news got out that you were the one to use the dart gun, we'd have to answer a lot of questions."

"Are you sure you're okay?" he asked.

She nodded, hating they had to resort to chemical capture. "These darts have enough anesthesia to immobilize Raja. I'll be fine. You and Wes get back."

Gemma backed up with them until she was behind a tree next to the main habitat building where they could run and hide if necessary. But the tranquilizer should only take a few seconds to kick in. Anger coursed through her at what had happened. But she shoved that out of the way. Cleared her thoughts. Focused her aim on Raja's hind limb. Her hand slicked against the dart gun as she pulled the trigger.

The dart went into Raja, giving Gemma a small sense of satisfaction, but it didn't counteract her guilt and fury over Raja's situation, especially when she watched the big cat groan and drop.

The next morning, Gemma nursed a large mug of black coffee in the kitchen, waiting for the others to arrive. Her head ached and she popped two ibuprofens. She'd already detailed the chores and schedules for the day on the whiteboard. Logged the previous night's incident in the notebook. Called the sheriff's office to report what had happened again.

The USDA inspection was a few days away. If she didn't find a way to stop this dangerous vandalism, someone was going to get hurt or killed. And, of course, she understood now that was the whole point. Someone wanted her to get hurt. Her, specifically—she was the target.

She thought she could build the sanctuary, under the new name of Tiger Mountain, into something as grand and glorious as the sanctuary her parents had run that had housed and cared for thirty animals. But, instead, someone wanted to shut down Tiger Mountain and wanted Gemma gone too, preferably dead. She could feel her dreams slipping away from her. Tiger Mountain slipping away.

Turning on the small wide-screen television mounted on the wall, she set it on the local news station but lowered the sound. She wasn't sure she could stomach very much noise this morning. She'd barely gotten any sleep last night and when she'd finally drifted off, her rest had been fitful at best. Too many questions running through her overactive mind.

Like why had Gray been there? He'd said he would explain, but he never had. She thought she could guess what his answer might be—that he was watching her, following her to make sure she was okay.

Gemma didn't know how she felt about that. She continued to have the eerie sense that someone watched her. Had it been Gray all this time? And who had left Raja's habitat open?

An image of a tiger on the television screen drew her attention. Gemma froze. In dismay, she stared.

She turned up the sound and watched in horror as photographs of Raja on the loose in the sanctuary filled the screen. "These pictures were taken just last night at the sanctuary known as Tiger Mountain, where a tiger apparently escaped and was on the loose for an undisclosed period of time," a reporter said, his face looming large in the TV screen. An investigative reporter had caught everything on camera? Who had he interviewed? How did he know?

The coffee mug slipped from her fingers and shattered on the floor.

EIGHT

Last night's incident still fresh in his mind, Gray parked his truck, a black Silverado and answered a call from Coop as he made his way to the Tiger Mountain facilities. He noted another vehicle parked in front of the main building.

"Saw the news this morning. You okay?"

Gray took a hesitant step and then stopped. "News? What news?"

"It's all over the news that a tiger got out last night at Tiger Mountain. There's some footage showing Gemma darting the tiger." Coop continued to explain, describing what the reporter had said about Gemma and Tiger Mountain and the supposed threat that the sanctuary presented to the local community.

Gray came close to swearing under his breath, but he bit back the words. That answered his biggest question—had it been an accident or planned? Of course, he'd suspected all along that it had been deliberate, but he hadn't had any definitive proof. Now it sounded like it had not only been planned but staged if a reporter was there to film the entire thing. Bile rose in his throat.

There's no way Gray had escaped being seen in the video. Had the reporter identified him? Was his cover blown? "Did you see me in the footage?"

"No. I know you're working undercover there, though."

Kicking a rock, Gray watched it roll across the still-moist ground. "I have to be in the footage. Most of the time, I was standing right next to Gemma. For part of it, when she got hurt, I was even carrying her. There's no way I could have escaped. The reporter saw me."

"But does he know who you really are? That's the big question."

"Maybe not. Why would he?" But if Sheriff Kruse looked at the entirety of the footage, then his cover would be blown, at least with the sheriff. Maybe that wouldn't be such a bad thing if he later required backup—which was possible since the situation kept getting more and more dangerous. But he needed more time to think about it. Needed to make sure no one within the department, like Deputy Callahan, for instance, was involved in any of the sabotage.

Gray wondered if the saboteur understood the risk of deliberately releasing Callie and Raja, or if they had intended to increase the danger. And with that thought, Gray had to question Kit's initial assessment and seriously consider that the vandalism and threats on Gemma's life could be connected. Committed by the same person or group. Regardless, someone wanted this sanctuary gone, even—or was it especially?—if that meant Gemma's life. It might be time for Gray to visit the neighboring rancher himself. Emil Atkins.

But he had to admit Wes was also suspect in the vandalism. He'd been there last night, though he claimed to have a reason. And while he might have been genuinely trying to help, his actions had definitely made the situation worse. Gemma wouldn't have needed to tranq Raja if it hadn't been for Wes.

But an even bigger question—what did any of this have to do with the trafficking ring he'd come here to investigate? Was there a connection? There were too many issues going on here. Did he refer once again to Occam's Razor, which would mean the simplest answer was the right one? That would suggest that only one entity was behind the vandalism, the attacks on Gemma's life and the trafficking ring. Could it be true?

All of these thoughts swirled in through his mind in a matter of seconds.

"Anything I can do to help?" Coop asked, pulling Gray from his thoughts.

Gray and Coop had their issues going all the way back to childhood, like all siblings did. Gray hated Cooper at times. Resented that their father favored him over Gray. But he'd made his peace with his brother, realizing that his issues with their father were between him and his father and were not the fault of anyone else. As adults, they'd left behind petty sibling rivalry and they had each other's back. Together, they watched over Alice, their only sister, and now Hadley, Coop's wife, was part of the family. After losing Jeremy, they only had each other. His suicide had brought them closer.

"Gray?" Coop's voice reminded Gray that he waited for an answer.

"No. Not yet. Your involvement at this juncture would raise too many questions."

"Okay then. Well, hurry and wrap this up so you can work your computer skills on this new system. Give me a Buck knife and throw me in the wilderness, and I'll survive just fine. Just don't put me in front of a computer accounting system."

Gray snorted.

"And Gray?"

"Yeah."

"Be careful."

"Always."

He ended the call, glad for the warning about the news, and headed to the resource building. It was still early but Gray couldn't sleep and he figured Gemma couldn't either. As he walked, he continued to chew over the questions about the previous evening's sabotage. Gray had already accepted that Raja's release had been deliberate rather than human error, especially with a news reporter ready and waiting, but had Gemma realized it? She had been fortunate Raja had been the tiger. Gray needed to think on that. Did that mean that whoever was threatening Gemma didn't work at Tiger Mountain, so the culprit wasn't familiar enough to expect Raja's positive reaction to Gemma? What had this person expected to happen? And what had the news crew come to see? Thrusting his cell into his pocket, he thought back to Cooper's call. Had Gemma even seen the news?

Finding it unlocked, he pressed through the front door and got the answer to his question.

Clyde hugged Gemma to him like a father would, comforting her. "We're going to overcome the bad press, Gemma. Don't you worry about it. This is why I'm here, and I'll stay as long as you need me to set things right. We'll find out who is behind this."

Gray felt awkward walking into the middle of

this. If he wasn't undercover, he would have excused himself and found something else to do. But he needed to be in the middle to make sure he didn't miss any vital information, so he waited where he was.

The man noticed Gray standing there, suspicion and anger pouring from his gaze. Gray wasn't sure any of it was meant for him, personally, but it was clear that Clyde was frustrated with what had happened. No matter that the man was suspected of running a huge trafficking ring—he also had sunk money into this sanctuary and, like any businessman, he wouldn't want to have it fail. Gray averted his gaze. Thinking of Clyde Morris involved in trafficking animal parts, and who knew what else, and as the guy also serving as the main venture capitalist behind a sanctuary twisted Gray's gut.

Clyde released Gemma, who wiped at her eyes. She turned them on Gray, surprise in her gaze. He held it. The sight of those big, clear hazel eyes—now red-rimmed—clawed at his heart. Whoever was doing this was going to answer to Gray. He would get Bill's killer, and he would get the person behind these attacks on Gemma and her tiger sanctuary.

But what he didn't know, what he couldn't be sure of, was it the same person behind it all?

"Gray." The one word—his name—was breathy

as it escaped her lips. She stepped forward. "Have you seen…" She trailed off as Gray nodded.

There was no need for her to complete the sentence. "The bad press, the way that reporter twisted the story to make it sound like Tiger Mountain is unsafe for any visitors, which you don't allow anyway, and for people living in the area? Yeah." He frowned. He hadn't seen it but he heard all he needed to hear from Coop. "It's scare tactics, trying to get people into a mob mind-set, too driven by fear to realize they're being manipulated to turn against you."

She shook her head, unshed tears in her eyes. "This could kill my efforts. Everything I've done so far. Everything we've done."

Clyde shifted. "All we need is some good press. Show some goodwill, public education. Anything to smooth things over."

"And we need to find who's behind this," Gray said. He eyed the kitchen down the hall behind them. He could use a strong cup of coffee to fuel his mind.

As if reading his thoughts, Gemma headed down the hallway. Clyde and Gray followed.

"I think we should let Wes go," Clyde said.

That news surprised Gray. In his undercover investigation, he'd tried to find out as much as he could about everyone working at Tiger Mountain.

Clyde had been the one to bring Wes on. Now he wanted to let him go?

Gemma poured Gray a cup. "I don't know. He could be completely innocent. My family has lived under suspicion and scrutiny for too long, and I don't want to live my life doing that to others—blaming them because of circumstantial evidence against them. The whole point of building Tiger Mountain—a whole new name with a fresh start—was to erase the past filled with suspicions." Her voice broke.

And snagged a little piece of Gray's heart. Over in the corner, he spotted a broom and pieces of a broken cup swept into a pile on the floor.

"You saw him talking to the neighbor, Gemma," Clyde said as he sugared his coffee. "And now this. We can't trust him. Just tell him we don't need him anymore."

Gray gulped too quickly and almost choked. "Wait, you saw him talking to the neighbor? The same man you believe is behind things?"

"There's more than one neighbor and I think they might even all be in it together, with him as their leader," Gemma admitted. "Emil hasn't made it a secret that he wants the sanctuary gone."

"I'm going to have a talk with him myself." Clyde slammed his cup on the table. "And the intern has to go."

"I can't afford to lose more help, Clyde. You know that."

"I'm not sure you can afford to keep him." Gray wasn't sure if Wes had played a role in anything, and he'd prefer to gather evidence against him or catch him in the act, but he wouldn't let Gemma remain in danger, if Wes was responsible. "I think Clyde is right."

"Thanks for your input." Clyde nodded, amusement in his eyes. Like Clyde was so secure in his certainty of Gemma's trust that it was funny to think of himself needing Gray's vote of confidence. "Which brings me to another question. What were you doing in the sanctuary last night, Gray?"

Oh, boy. Gemma had asked him the same question and he had put her off because he had to focus on securing the tiger, but he had hoped to explain himself to Gemma alone. "I won't lie. I wanted to be the hero. I thought I could watch the sanctuary at night. Keep an eye out and wait for whoever is causing the problems—catch them in the act."

Was Gray holding his breath, waiting for Clyde's reaction? For Gemma's? He released it slowly, so they wouldn't notice. And now if Clyde was the man he'd been hunting, he'd just revealed his surveillance, and maybe even lost any chance he'd have of catching him in illicit activity.

Finally, Clyde nodded. "And your actions saved Gemma's life."

"It was Raja, Clyde. I would have been fine."

"Not with that idiot Wes spraying the cat with water. Gray was there to help you. Thanks for taking care of my Gemma." There was something more behind the man's eyes, but Gray wouldn't say it was gratitude.

Gray fought to read it, to understand the look there. Was he playing with Gray? Toying with him? Like a cat might play with a lizard he caught before killing it?

Other staff began to mosey in, grabbing coffee as needed. Cara entered the kitchen and hugged Gemma. Questions arose about the incident. Most were relieved all had ended well, but Gray didn't miss the wariness in their eyes.

He left Gemma with the volunteers and headed to the sanctuary grounds to search for clues. He'd leave the compound before anyone from the sheriff's office arrived to investigate that someone had purposefully left the tiger's habitat open. He hoped they'd question that reporter too. Eventually, Gray would have to make contact with Sheriff Kruse and share what he knew, but Gray would avoid that as long as he could. Gemma needed the support of the sheriff's department now and bringing his investigation into the mix—an investigation in which Gemma, on paper, still looked like a viable suspect—would just confuse matters.

That evening, Gray went to the nearest Laundromat to wash a load of clothes. Working at the wildlife sanctuary had him burning through two sets of clothes a day. Laundry had never been something he enjoyed doing, but he had to admit that he was glad for this downtime to sort through his thoughts. This investigation had turned into something much different than he'd expected. All he could think about was helping Gemma and Tiger Mountain. His thoughts had moved far from what they were when he'd first arrived.

He stuffed quarters into the drier, hoping he'd be out of here in the next thirty minutes. Was he losing sight of the real goal? His main purpose here? When his supervisor, Mark, called, Gray wasn't sure he was ready to talk to him and almost let the call go to voice mail.

But he answered and stepped outside into the starry night to talk in private. "Yeah."

"There's been an arrest made for the sale of tiger parts."

What? "When?"

"This morning. We believe it's connected to your trafficking ring. No way for you to be in more than one place at a time, Gray, so don't beat yourself up."

Gray hadn't made the arrest and it burned him.

This was his investigation. Frustration grated him. "Why arrest the guy? If I'm about to close in on the head of the ring, I don't want him running scared off to some other country."

"The sale was made in Chicago, far removed from your suspect. It couldn't be ignored. The agent couldn't let it go. But I don't think you need to worry. Maybe your guy will make a few mistakes if he gets nervous."

He ended the call. Mark's words should put him back on track. With this arrest and the increased incidents, pressure building up at Tiger Mountain, Gray could sense his time was running out. The person he was after might back off or disappear completely before he could gather the evidence to catch them in the act.

Unfortunately, Clyde hadn't made any suspicious moves. Yet. But Gray now had two diametrically opposed goals—to keep Gemma safe as he helped her save Tiger Mountain and to bring down Clyde, the venture capitalist behind the sanctuary. How could he do both?

Gray returned to the Laundromat and found a guy stuffing his clothes into a sack. "What... what are you doing, man? Those are my clothes!"

The guy shrugged. "I thought you left them and weren't coming back."

"I was right outside, dude." Frowning, Gray snatched the sack from the guy and made sure all the clothes had been scraped from the drier. "Of course you knew I was coming. I wouldn't leave my clothes behind."

The guy was an opportunist, that was all—looking to get as much as he could, without sparing a thought for the well-being of anyone else. If Clyde was truly the one responsible for the trafficking ring, then he was the same way. Benefiting from the tigers without a thought of how he was harming either the rare and precious creatures themselves or Gemma, who he claimed to love like a daughter and who would defend those tigers with her life.

Shaking his head, Gray headed out the door.

Climbing into his truck, something else wound through his thoughts.

Gemma would defend the tigers with her life...

He popped the steering wheel and sat back. Clyde was after what he could get—and that meant the tiger parts that he could sell to the highest bidder. If that was the goal, it seemed that whoever was behind the threats on Gemma and the harassment—the same person to call the investigative reporter—didn't want the sanctuary gone. They wanted Gemma gone one way or another in order to leave the tigers unprotected.

And then, he had the connection he needed between the sabotage, the attempts on her life and the trafficking ring.

Either she would leave on her own, fed up with the harassment and struggles.

Or she would stay and die.

Standing at the utility closet in one of the habitat's indoor facilities, Gemma absently selected a broom as she glanced at the text she'd sent a few minutes ago and Gray's ready response:

I'll be right there.

Had she been right to text him and ask him to meet her? Being alone wasn't safe, as he'd repeatedly warned her and now she finally agreed. She'd said goodbye to Cara as she'd left, and Gemma had headed to the habitat to make sure the tigers were safe. One last time.

God, please don't let anyone tamper with things.

Though she'd prayed the silent prayer in her heart, she didn't expect a response. The prayer had been a desperate cry for help as the overwhelming feeling she was about to lose everything she'd worked for weighed on her.

Nor could she leave the heaviness behind, especially when it wasn't safe to even walk the sanctuary grounds or a trail in the woods alone. So she needed protection.

An image of Gray—his wide shoulders and

warm, brown eyes—had popped into her head so she'd texted him.

Part of her wanted him to be here with her to help protect the sanctuary from those who wanted it gone. But, if she was honest with herself, she also wanted to see Gray for reasons that had nothing to do with that. Even though she hadn't known him long, there was something about him that made her feel safe. Add to that—was she making a list?—that he had a sense of purpose about him that she liked and admired. Gray had also mentioned he had ideas about public education. With everything that had happened, they had hardly had time to sit down and discuss his ideas. Or maybe Gemma was only now desperate enough to admit she needed his help. She was willing to listen to ideas from an outsider because, with the current bad press, Tiger Mountain was at a critical juncture. She'd had a PR brainstorming meeting this morning with Clyde, but even he seemed preoccupied and they'd come up with the usual, tired ideas that left them both unenthusiastic.

Needing to work, she flipped on the rest of the lights in the building that served four tigers, disturbing Raja, who had abandoned his chuffing from last night for angry groans today. Maybe she should have picked a different building to work in, but she desperately wanted the tiger to trust her again.

The whole incident had left Gemma feeling sick to her stomach.

But that's why she was here now. She couldn't sit around with so many frustrating thoughts converging on her. She needed to be proactive. Gemma had experienced trials and tribulations in her life and she'd never been one to give up.

But now...now she didn't know how much more she could take.

At least there was a bit of good news. Caesar was old and had issues, but the vet had confirmed he didn't have liver cancer, so they could expect him to stay around a few more years.

A noise startled her. Her heart jumped. Gray's sturdy form stepped into the hallway that ran next to the tiger stalls. He'd made pretty good time. Had only taken him fifteen minutes to get here. "Hey, I wish you would have waited for me before you came here alone."

She wouldn't tell him she'd already been here when she'd texted. "I'll try to remember that next time." As if there would be more of these meetings with him.

He tugged off his black jacket, revealing a tan polo shirt that stretched tight over his broad chest.

Looking good, better than a man had a right to, he jammed his hands into his jeans and strode toward her, glancing at the broom in her hands. "Are we cleaning? Or are we going to talk about my ideas?"

"Can't we do both?"

He chuckled. "Sure. But it seems to me you've already had a long, exhausting day, not to mention last night."

Gemma sagged. It didn't take a brain surgeon to know that she was tired, but, still, she felt like Gray understood her. And that pushed her to be a bit more honest in her reply than she otherwise might have been. "I have to keep busy. It helps me to get my mind off things. I want to hear all your ideas about educating the public. We have a lot of work to do." She huffed and then glanced to him. "I say *we*, but you're only a volunteer. I don't mean to assume you'll want to put so much time and energy into saving Tiger Mountain." She'd said the words, but could he see her desperate pleas for help reflecting in her eyes?

He grabbed the broom, his hand pressing over hers. "Gemma."

The way his gaze searched hers, Gemma felt like he'd caressed her. Emotion welled up, taking her breath away. Stepping back, she released the broom to him. But Gray stepped forward, staying close.

"I'll do whatever you want or need done to

help keep Tiger Mountain going. I hope by now you believe me."

Still grappling with the whirl of emotions that his nearness stirred, she said, "I don't know how much more of this I can take, but, maybe with your help, I can…"

"Gemma. If only—" He lifted his hand as though he might cup her cheek and then dropped it. "But there's more going on here than just the need to keep the sanctuary going. Something sinister and dangerous. I'm more worried about your safety. I don't know if you should stay here at all."

"I know what you're doing. You're backing out on me, aren't you?" She'd already lost volunteers and staffers over the last few weeks and months.

"What?" He frowned. "I didn't say that. There's something I need to tell—" Gray suddenly frowned, his gaze shifting to something beyond her.

"What's the matter?" she asked.

Gray gently urged Gemma to move behind him. "I'm not sure."

Someone else was there, or at least had been there, tampering again. She just knew it. Fear and anger surged through her. She wanted to rush around Gray and see what was going on. See who was behind all her troubles. "Well, what are you waiting on?"

"Just…listen."

Craning her neck, she tried to see as well as listen. What had Gray heard that had him tensing? Grabbing his side? Was he somehow injured last night?

"Oh no!" Gray rushed forward. "Stay close to me!"

"What…" But her words dropped away when she saw the orange and yellow flickers through the glass window of the door to the room where they stored supplies and processed meals for the tigers. The pungent scent of acrid smoke reached her nose.

NINE

Flames licked higher on the other side of the door. The sight momentarily stunned Gray. Low groans and frantic growls echoed through the shelter from the tigers who'd come indoors for the evening.

Gray's own panic rose. They had to put the fire out. He followed Gemma. On the wall hung an extinguisher. Or where a fire extinguisher should have been. Gemma glanced at him. "It's…gone."

Go figure.

He pursed his lips, fear and anger boiling inside. Gray peeked through the window into the room. How could the fire have grown so fast without some sort of accelerant? That, and the absent extinguisher, pointed to the conclusion that someone had planned this. "We have to get out of here."

"The animals!"

"We need to call 911 to get the fire department here."

Wild with fear, Gemma's eyes held him in place. As if that wasn't enough, she gripped the collar of his shirt. "They're too far away. What if they don't make it in time?"

"You can't panic, Gemma. These animals are depending on you."

Nodding her agreement, she stood tall and determined and then started checking that all the habitats were open to the outside, which they normally should have been. But this situation was far from normal. All things considered, if someone had started this fire, there was the possibility they had locked the tigers in. Gemma must have been thinking the same thing. Then she moved to each caged stall, making sure each tiger had fled, and closed the cage doors to lock them out. They had all fled except for Caesar, the geriatric tiger.

Gray would have assisted her to speed the process, but when he got a signal on his phone—always difficult in this area—he remained in place so he wouldn't lose it and dialed the number. Her face reflected her distress as she tried to urge the old tiger to get up and move outside, away from the very real danger.

Each ring of the phone—as Gray waited for someone on the other end of the emergency number to answer—seemed to take an eternity. Why was it taking so long? He watched Gemma as she tried to urge Caesar outside, using a clicker.

Finally, dispatch answered.

Gray started right in. "There's a fire at Tiger Mountain at Habitat B." The county fire department should have the detailed information regarding the layout of the tiger sanctuary. After answering a few more questions, Gray ended the call.

"I can't get Caesar to move."

"He'll move, Gemma. It's instinctive, pure and simple."

Appearing unconvinced, she pursed her lips. Other than being the oldest tiger in the sanctuary, was Caesar hurting or injured in a way that made him unable to exit the stall?

The stakes had just grown higher if they couldn't get Caesar out. "What is the fire escape plan?"

They hadn't been over that important detail yet, though he'd been told it was reviewed once a month at the weekly staff meeting. Gray hadn't been here that long.

"Prevention, detection and suppression, in that order." Gemma headed to the door that separated them from the fire. The fire had grown and would soon choke them out of this room before the flames even got to them.

"And if none of that works?" Gray asked.

Gemma coughed and covered her mouth and nose. "Their outdoor habitats should be enough space for the cats to stay safe unless things get out of hand."

None of that mattered for Caesar if he was unable to get far enough away. And as for the other big cats, if Gray and Gemma didn't get control and the fire began burning the habitats, then what? There was one reason to be thankful for all the rain they'd received this season. He hoped the wetter-than-normal conditions would be enough to slow the fire.

"And if it does get out of hand?"

She glowered at him. "It won't. But worst case, the fencing surrounding the entire sanctuary could keep the tigers in, if we're forced to release the animals from even their outside habitats. It would be better to have the others here to help transfer them to cages and transport them to the other side of the sanctuary or away from the danger. I'll text Cara and ask her to round up some help, but we don't have time to wait. We can use the hose and pump from the pond."

Agreed. "Then hurry. Let's get out of here." A sense of dread snaked up his spine. It wasn't going to be as simple as that, especially if this was arson. This fire had been planned, staged to burn hot, fast and out of control. It wouldn't be easily contained.

"But what about Caesar?"

"We have to trust he'll move, but in the meantime we have to put out the fire." He grabbed her hand to pull her through the door as he pushed against the exit.

Locked.

Gemma's pulse spiked even higher. But she couldn't let panic set in. Keeping her head would make the difference between life and death.

"Over there." She led him as they ran to the opposite end. "There are three exits in this building. Something has to be open."

Right. The door Gray had just walked through was now locked. She'd been an idiot to let this happen. They tried the other door. Also locked. And the third door was now engulfed in flames.

Gray eyed Gemma. "Can we unlock them?"

"There's no way to do that from the inside. Why would there be?" Gemma's eyes and throat burned. They'd definitely need to rethink the locks on these buildings in the future in case someone was trapped inside. Whoever did this had known they would be locked inside with no escape.

Smoke began filling the room, sneaking beneath the crack of the door from the room engulfed in flames. At this rate, the smoke would overcome them long before the flames reached them.

"The habitats." Gray paced next to the bars,

reminding her of the tigers. "We go out through one of the habitats."

"That could put us in harm's way from the cats."

"Take your pick. Either way, we're in danger. For certain, we'll die in here. We have to take our chances with the tigers."

"It's dangerous, but you're right. I don't see another way out."

"But which tiger?" He started opening an enclosure.

"No, wait," she said. "Let's go out with Caesar. We can coax him out and he's not likely to hurt us. He's relatively tame by comparison to some of the others. He's been with us almost as long as Raja and I think he'll understand we only want to help."

Gray's eyes widened. "I don't know, Gemma. The only time I've been that close to him he was sedated for the vet. He's huge."

"Like size would matter. Even the smallest one here could take you out with one swat. Besides, we need to get him out of here. He isn't moving. You said we should go out through the tiger stalls—now let's go. It's the only way."

Coughs racked Gemma as she made her way toward Caesar's stall. "You go out one of the other habitats and you'll be taking your chances with more dangerous animals. Caesar is older and weaker and he trusts me." Though she didn't make it a regular practice to pet the animals—Tiger Mountain was about being a true sanctuary and creating a natural environment—there had to be a measure of trust between the big cats and their caretakers.

"Caesar it is."

The flames had conquered the door and now climbed the walls. Heat flashed over her and smoke billowed. Gray nodded and followed Gemma. She gently spoke to Caesar, slowly entering his stall and letting the big cat know she was coming into his space. Despite the training she'd given him to receive care and feeding, she had never been with him in the stall. That was simply too dangerous.

Caesar released long, low moans but made no effort to move. That concerned her as much as the fire. Why hadn't he moved out on his own, instinctively distancing himself from the fire? Gray started into the stall, but she gestured for him to wait.

"Let me lead him out first. He doesn't know you like he knows me."

"You'd better hurry if we're going to get to the hose and save anything in this habitat, including ourselves and Caesar."

Gemma had her clicker in her pocket as always, and she stepped out of the stall into the outside of Caesar's habitat. If only she had some food with her. She clicked three times and waited just outside of the door. Beyond the cage, Gray coughed. She had to hurry.

"Come on, Caesar. We need to get you some place safe." Three more clicks and Caesar growled and grumbled but in a nonthreatening way, and then he got up and lumbered out the door. "Good boy, Caesar. Good boy."

This wasn't a circus, and Gemma didn't pet the old cat on his head or rub his ears as she'd done with Raja last night. That had been under completely different circumstances. She hadn't told Gray, but Raja might have attacked him had she not drawn the big cat's attention and relied on his familiarity with her. It had been a calculated ploy on her part. There was no need to take further risks with Caesar, especially given that the fire could have already set him on edge.

"Gemma," Gray called. "I'm coming through."

Gray had already entered and left the stall. He headed for the gate of the habitat, the exit into the sanctuary at large. Gemma wanted to lure Caesar farther away from the building in flames. She glanced at Gray. He waited by the gate, a question in his eyes.

Should he get the hose now and start putting out the flames? Was Gemma okay alone in the habitat with Caesar?

She nodded. *Go. I'll be okay.*

As soon as she knew Caesar was safe, she'd see to her own safety and exit the habitat so she could help Gray. Now that Caesar was up and moving, he didn't need much encouragement to continue to the far end of his enclosure. He slowly lumbered away, disappearing into the grass.

Relief swooshed through her for Caesar, but one glance back at the flames and her heart tumbled over itself.

Gemma was more grateful than ever that the enclosures were large and spacious, giving the animals plenty of room to roam and, in this case, to be far from the flames. She hoped and prayed the volunteer fire department would soon arrive with their truck filled with two thousand gallons of water and put out the flames before the animals were harmed. The building itself was another story.

The flames were quickly dashing her hope they could salvage most of the structure. Another glance at the area where she'd last seen Caesar reassured her he was safe for now. She headed to the gate so she could help Gray bring in the water hose. In the distance, beneath a security light, she spotted him already going toward the building. Determined to beat the flames, she picked up her pace, hating her cane now like never before.

Glancing toward the building, she watched the

hot glow of the fire escaping the structure light up the night.

And across the way, she saw a figure slip out of the ring of light into the shadows.

TEN

Holding the hose, Gray doused the flames, grateful for the water pressure, but he doubted his efforts would be enough. In the distance, lights flashed as emergency vehicles headed up the road into the property. Other vehicle headlights followed, likely bringing the other staffers to help.

God, please let it be so.

Where was Gemma? Had she secured Caesar yet?

To his relief, he saw her silhouette rushing toward him with her cane, the inferno at her back.

Bending over her knees, she caught her breath. "I saw… I saw someone." She pointed to the other side of the building. "Just over there. He ran away. Do you hear me, Gray? Someone was there and then ran into the shadows."

"Did you see who it was?"

"No…" She gulped a few more breaths and then finally stood tall. "It was just a figure. A glimpse of someone. They stepped into the shadows as though they knew I had seen them. Maybe I'm getting paranoid. I started to search—"

"No!" Gray almost handed the hose over to Gemma so he could search, but he wouldn't leave her alone with the flames. He wouldn't leave her alone, period. "No, it's too dangerous. Whoever it was, they probably started the fire. It's too risky to try to corner someone who's willing to go to such insane lengths. That's why it's important that you try to think, try to remember if you recognized them."

The fire truck finally arrived. The firemen steered it all the way up into the sanctuary through double gates thrown wide open. One of the Tiger Mountain staffers must have opened it for them. Gray continued using the hose, spraying the flames as well as the rest of the building and the animal habitats to protect them, unconcerned about depleting the pond water, considering all the rain they'd received. But when he realized he was standing in the way of the more experienced firemen, he turned off his hose and moved to the side. He stood back and watched with Gemma and the others—Cara, Tom, Jill, Mavis and Ernie—who had arrived. Clyde had supposedly released Wes from his service at Tiger Mountain earlier in the day. They all stood, looking on in horror.

Everyone except Clyde. He wasn't here.

Gray leaned in to whisper. "Does Clyde know?"

She nodded. "I texted him. But if I remember correctly, he's in Portland. Cara called the others. They're all here, except...except for Wes, of course."

Gemma hadn't wanted to let him go.

She put one hand over her mouth and crossed her arm over her body. Her eyes glistened with unshed tears. "This is the absolute worst thing that could happen. The worst. I don't understand why this is happening. This will be a huge setback."

"Yeah, not to mention the cleanup. We could barely keep on top of caring for the tigers in the first place." Anger flashed in Tom's gaze.

Cara shot him a glare, but it went unnoticed by Gemma. This wasn't the time to complain about the extra work that would be needed to restore the habitat and to reassure the animals agitated by the chaos and flames.

"It's not the worst thing, Gemma," Gray said. "The flames will be put out before they can harm any of the tigers. It could have been much worse." But he wasn't sure his reassurances helped much.

Still, the animals might not be physically harmed, but they had to be distressed by the smell of smoke, sensing the danger. Their growls and pacing confirmed it. From here Gray could tell that at least two of the stalls had been consumed by flames. A few more minutes of burning unchecked and the fire would have hit the lush foliage in the outdoor habitats. Some of it was still wet, but the sun and wind had dried out the trees and grasses.

He thought of the figure Gemma claimed to have seen stepping deeper into the shadows. Fury blew through his veins. Gray grabbed a flashlight from Tom. He'd bet that figure was the arsonist, and he stomped off to search.

"Where are you going?" Gemma limped after him.

"Stay here. You need to stay with the staff and keep safe."

"You're going to look for him, aren't you?"

"Him, Gemma? So you saw at least that much?"

"I—I think it was a guy, yes. That was my first impression. Is that where you're going? To look for him?"

"Yes. And I want you to stay here."

Had it been Emil Atkins or Wes, whom she had recently let go? What about Clyde? Sure, he was supposedly out of town, but Gray wouldn't believe that alibi without proof. No matter who it was, Gray was determined to find him. But had he already wasted too much time? Maybe the guy had fled the scene. It was possible, but he doubted it. The arsonist would likely want to hang around to watch the show and view the damage he'd created.

Gray took off, heading in the direction where Gemma had pointed moments before. He heard her efforts to keep up with him and hated himself. All he had to do to lose her was start running, but that would be completely heartless. He slowed and turned to face her.

Eyes blazing, she caught up to him.

"What are you doing, Gemma? It's dark and dangerous, and…and…" He could make better time without her. But he wouldn't say the words.

"I want to find him. I want to know who did this. I want this to end." She nearly broke then, as her voice cracked, but she didn't lose her composure in front of him.

So strong and beautiful, even when her life was in upheaval. Gray could hardly stand to watch her go through it.

He couldn't help himself. He closed the distance between them and wrapped her in his arms. "You don't always have to be so strong, you know?"

A shudder ran through her. Was she crying? Releasing her pent-up anxiety and fury? Whatever it was, Gray sensed Gemma needed him to hold her. She needed human contact and, if he was honest with himself, he did too. He lifted his hand and felt the softness of her long and luscious hair.

She pressed her face against his shoulder. An image of Clyde holding her in a similar fashion flashed through him, but this was not a friendly, fatherly—or even brotherly—hug. No. With Gemma in his arms, his protective nature ignited more fiercely than he could have imagined even as he struggled to ignore the attraction he had for this woman. But it was more than that. Comforting her, keeping her safe, had warmth swimming around his heart and he knew he cared for her in a deeper way. He wanted something lasting with her.

But he couldn't let that longing go any further. He forced his attention onto the damaged building. Reminded of why he was here working undercover at Tiger Mountain.

He noted the flames were finally out at the building. Gemma seemed to sense a change in the atmosphere and she stepped back from him but not too far. He still held her. "If I'm not strong, who will be? Who will take care of these tigers? Who will build the legacy that should have belonged to my parents?"

He understood her then. Even with Clyde's support, she thought she was all alone in her efforts to build something lasting and good. In that moment Gray wanted to tell her everything. Who he was and why he was really here. She was so open in that moment that it made him feel low and petty for ever lying to her or keeping anything from her. Gray wanted to join Gemma in her cause. They were on the same side, after all— to protect endangered and abused animals from evil, wicked men. What could it hurt to tell her everything?

He was letting her get to him. With the moonlight shining brightly in her eyes, he had the strange desire to kiss her. Kiss away her worries like they were in some fairy tale.

Right. Like that would work in real life. Gray drew in a breath, catching the fetid scent of the water-soaked, charred building. Good. Reality was coming back to him. He remembered why he'd come to stand here. He wanted to find the arsonist. The man standing in the shadows.

The dark forest of the Wild Rogue Wilderness loomed behind them, and the back of his neck tingled.

Someone was watching them.

The next day Gemma wasn't sure how she would have pulled her heartbroken, aching body out of bed, if it wasn't for the animals who depended on her. She'd gotten up before dawn so she could be ready to give special attention to all the tigers today. Her nerves were on edge at the thought of the damage she would see once the morning sun illuminated last night's disaster.

She detailed the chores and schedules on the whiteboard and found she could use an additional one. There was simply too much to do. Still, she did her best so that no one would have any questions about what should be done or what she expected from them. She wished Clyde hadn't let Wes go. She could use his help.

She held on to a sliver of hope that some people in the community would assist with the cleanup, but first, the cause of the fire had to be investigated. She and Gray had shared what they knew with the firemen last night.

Gemma had always thought of herself as a positive person. Someone who chose to take the proverbial lemons and make lemonade, despite the many hurdles life had thrown in her path. But she couldn't deny that her positivity had been running on fumes. And now this—a fire set to trap her and Gray inside and either burn them alive or force them into the habitats with the tigers, where they faced death of a different kind. She struggled to keep from crumbling. Who wouldn't give up under such circumstances? She wanted to keep strong and stay the course, but her confidence had been shaken.

If she could just hold on until the sheriff learned who was behind these attacks, then Tiger Mountain could go forward. To that end, she thought about the tigers and their need for a home.

Somehow, they would be ready for the fast approaching USDA inspection that would give her the ability to continue forward. She could only hope they would overlook the decimated habitat.

And Clyde would encourage her when he got here. He always did. And there was someone else, someone unexpected, who encouraged her now as well.

Gray.

The thought of him filled her with warmth and left her confused.

The front door opened and shut. Gemma glanced over from the whiteboard and spotted Clyde ambling toward her, his shoulders slumped. Defeat in his expression.

Gemma absently put the marker aside, the look in Clyde's eyes scaring her. "Clyde?"

He placed his hands on her shoulders. "I'm so sorry I wasn't there to help you last night."

"It's okay. You said you were in Portland. You can't be two places at once."

"I was raising funds for Tiger Mountain." He hung his head.

"What is it? What's wrong?" Gemma sensed more had gone wrong than just the fire.

"I know this is going to be hard for you to

hear, but, with this setback, we're going to have to downsize."

"What do you mean?" Gemma held her breath.

"Not for long. Just until we can get this behind us. I've already arranged for two tigers to be moved to another sanctuary."

Gemma stepped away from him, causing him to drop his hands.

"Now, Gemma, you know it's the only way. We've lost an entire habitat building. How are you going to manage the tigers otherwise?"

"We have the extra habitat that we use for rotation."

"And then our standard of care drops and they all suffer."

He was right. She had been holding on to false hope. She wasn't sure how she felt that he'd made this decision without even discussing it with her. But he was her benefactor and silent partner. Older, wiser and more experienced. Who was she to challenge him?

"Let me think about the tigers, then. Which two are better suited for travel and more able to adapt to a new environment. Kayla is young and healthy and hasn't been with us long enough to feel a sense of loss. And there's Sierra…"

Clyde grabbed her hand to stop her pacing. "Caesar, Gemma. Caesar costs us a lot of time and money. And Raja. It'll be better for our public image if he's gone—the community sees him as a threat after the news story of him running loose."

Heart crashing against her chest, she yanked her hand away. "You already decided? These are my decisions to make. Clyde, I know these animals better than you do. Moving Caesar to a new environment at this stage in his life will be too hard on him. No—" She shook her head "—I won't allow it."

His mouth flatlined, his face morphing from compassionate to stern. "The decision has already been made. And tell no one else. I don't want the drama."

Clyde turned and walked out.

What?

She gulped for air. What had just happened? As Clyde exited, Cara walked through the door, followed by Ernie and Mavis, their faces grim. It was up to Gemma to project a positive can-do attitude. Tiger Mountain depended on it. A dark cloud of depression and hopelessness loomed over her, but she kept it at bay. Standing tall, she welcomed everyone and went over the duties she'd outlined on the whiteboard.

"We can't do a lot in the way of cleanup until the fire investigator gives us the go-ahead, but we can tend to the tigers like it's any other day until then." She smiled, hoping the act would bring her heart around.

Gemma was disappointed that Gray hadn't joined the morning crew. Hadn't she just been thinking that he encouraged her? That's what she got for counting on someone. She knew better than to rely on anyone besides herself and Clyde. "Anyone know if Gray is coming in?" And now she'd asked about him.

"I saw him in the sanctuary," Cara said. "I think he's looking things over."

A measure of relief lifted her spirits. She'd misjudged him.

"Thanks for letting me know. I'll join you guys in a few minutes." She nodded her dismissal.

Cara led everyone outdoors to get busy with the usual chores. Gemma just needed a moment alone to gather her composure. But the truth was she was postponing the moment when she would see the damage in the light of day. Clyde's pronouncement that he was letting two tigers to go to another facility hadn't helped her frame of mind. Her leg throbbed like never before, forcing her to admit the stress came close to overwhelming her.

The man had been like family but while he was like a father to her in some ways, in others he was more like a distant relative. He had only planned to be here for a few weeks and then he would be gone again to work on foreign soil regarding his wildlife preservation efforts.

And then… Gemma would be alone again.

Abandoned. The fact that someone wanted her dead drove the loneliness into her marrow.

Life shouldn't be so hard, should it? She was trying to do a good thing in this world.

She stared at the whiteboard, which was covered in so much ink you couldn't exactly call it white anymore.

It's not about me. If I just put my thoughts and energy into the sanctuary and into those working with me, then I won't be lonely.

There. She couldn't procrastinate any longer. To the sanctuary, then, to get her work done and view the damage done by last night's fire.

Someone came through the door just as Gemma put aside the marker. She turned to see Gray striding toward her. Her heart tripped, if only a little. Strange how he always seemed to show up when she was feeling down. He'd been there that day on the trail when she'd been frustrated and wanted time to think. It was like he sensed when she needed him. But that was ridiculous. Absurd! And she couldn't think about him like that. Of all the people she worked with, she knew Gray the least.

Then why did she find herself wanting to trust him?

Arms crossed, giving her a glimpse of his well-developed biceps, he stood near and studied her, his downturned mouth shifting into a half grin.

"Don't look so sad, Gemma. It's going to be okay. You'll see. We're all going to pitch in."

Those were the words she'd expected to hear from Clyde. "What are you doing here?"

It was obvious he'd come in search of her, but she wanted to know why.

"I thought I'd walk with you to see the damage."

"But you've already seen it, haven't you?" Gemma remembered Cara telling her earlier.

"Yes." He offered a hand. "And, now, I'm going back with you to see it."

Gray was the one to reassure her and to build her confidence this time. Not Clyde. Gemma, normally the positive one, was now the one who needed coaxing to face the day.

Unsure why, she slipped her hands into his reassuring grip. Her breath caught. Ridiculous. "Is it…is it bad?"

"It could have been much worse. So while you're viewing the damage, remember the tigers survived and you will simply rebuild. The habitats can be replaced. You care about the tigers and it's why you saved them. It's what I like about you."

What he liked about her? Why should his confession send warm tingles through her? Tingles and warning signals. And yet, she left her hand in his as he led her out and into the sanctuary, up the hill toward the damaged habitat. Smoke still tainted the air, but the sun shone with the promise of a new start. If she tried, Gemma could imagine a bright future. This was just another hurdle. The sheriff would find the culprit and the sabotage would end. Tiger Mountain would pass the inspection. That day couldn't come soon enough. She allowed a ray of happiness to brighten her mood.

Gray slowed until he stopped. "The sheriff is here."

Good—the sooner he found a lead for his investigation, the faster this could all be resolved. But then she heard a deep, guttural scream that sliced through her hope.

"Come, quick. Over here!" someone yelled. It was Cara.

Gray hurried along with Gemma. She knew she slowed him down with her cane, but she was grateful he didn't let her go. Near the woods where she'd seen someone in the shadows lay Wes's body.

ELEVEN

Why had he lied to Gemma? Everything wasn't going to be okay no matter how many people pitched in. With Wes's murder, things had spiraled from bad to worse.

Gray marched through the door into Sheriff Kruse's office and shut it behind him.

The sheriff looked up in surprise. "Well, well, well, Special Agent Gray Wilde. What brings you here?"

"You need to interview all the volunteers and staff at Tiger Mountain, don't you?"

The sheriff's brows rose and then flattened. "Yes, why?"

"I'm one of the volunteers. Gray Wilson."

Slowly, the sheriff nodded his head. "Now I understand why Mr. Wilson was so sneaky and got away from the sanctuary before I could question him. I heard he went to search the woods where Gemma had seen someone last night. Now we've found a body. Sounds awfully suspicious to me."

"May I?" Gray gestured at one of two chairs in the sheriff's sparse office.

"Go ahead. Make yourself comfortable. How about some coffee to go along with your story, which I'm sure is going to be a good one."

The man's sarcasm rang through loud and clear. He hadn't appreciated that Gray's brother, Cooper Wilde, had taken it on himself to protect a woman being chased by an assassin and hadn't bothered to contact the sheriff on the matter earlier that year. The truth was that Cooper had tried, but the department was spread too thin, and there hadn't been time to wait on their response. Add to that, the sheriff suspected Gray had known about the woman's situation and kept it to himself—which was partially true. He had helped his brother when Coop had called him, even though he hadn't been told all the details. But, seriously, had the sheriff thought he and his department had the skills to face an actual international assassin entangled in CIA affairs?

"No thanks on the coffee." Gray eased into the chair. He had to choose his words carefully. The last thing he wanted to do was plant suspicions that sheriff would then direct at Gemma. "I'm working undercover at Tiger Mountain."

Sheriff Kruse poured himself coffee as he considered his reply. "Care to share more than that with me? I might know something that can help."

He sat and then leaned back in the chair as he drank.

Scratching his jaw, Gray thought about how much he should share. He didn't want the sheriff interfering, but neither did he want the man tracking him down because he hadn't been questioned. The timing on this couldn't have been worse.

"I got some intel that said someone at Tiger Mountain is involved in wildlife trafficking. Specifically tiger parts. I'm sure you're aware how much money that can bring in."

"A wildlife sanctuary involved in trafficking. Haven't heard that one before."

Gray recognized that the man was baiting him. He chose not to take the bait. He wasn't going to share what he'd learned about Gemma's partner, Clyde Morris.

"Look, I can't really tell you more than that. Please just give me the space to work."

"And the threats on Gemma's life? What do they have to do with your investigation?"

He hesitated. "I—I can't be sure yet. She believes her neighbors would like the sanctuary gone, but I think someone wants her out of the picture completely because she is too close to the tigers and it's hard to move the animals when someone cares like she does." Now, why had he gone on about her like that?

"Sounds like she isn't the only one who cares." Sheriff Kruse lifted a brow.

When Gray said nothing, the sheriff leaned forward and put his elbows on his desk. "What about her safety, Gray? I need to investigate who murdered Wes Stimpson, and also learn who is trying to kill Gemma. How am I supposed to give you space?"

"Keep your investigation restricted to the murder and the attempt on her life." Frowning, Gray leaned forward too. "But any investigation is likely to interfere with mine or speed up timetables. I think things are about to go down soon."

"Let me know if there is anything I can do to help. But I do know something that might be important."

"Yeah?"

"Wes has a sister who's ill. She needs surgery that will cost far more money than the family can pay even with insurance. They've been trying to raise funds. It was on the local news."

Gray listened, wondering what else the sheriff had to add.

"I talked to the mother, gave her the news this morning of his death."

"I'm sorry."

"Part of the job, but it doesn't make it easier. She told me she'd heard him talking about the tigers and how much the parts could bring."

Stunned, Gray sat back. Wes? He couldn't be heading up a trafficking ring, could he? No, he was too young—this ring had been in place since before Bill's investigation started all those years ago. Wes would have been just a kid at the time. This didn't make sense.

"Of course, she scolded him for talking like that, she said. And then, apparently, he was released from working at the sanctuary. Hours later, someone tries to burn down one of the habitats. I'd say Wes did it. He had no legitimate reason to be there, and it wouldn't be surprising if he held a grudge after being released. But if he set the fire, then who killed him?"

Gray didn't like the insinuation in his tone. As if Gray had anything to do with it. "So he *was* murdered."

"The ME strongly suspects his death wasn't accidental but I haven't seen the report yet.

Gray nodded. "We can work together to find out."

The sheriff studied him.

Maybe Wes had learned something he wasn't supposed to know about the trafficking ring. If he was talking tiger parts, that would make sense.

He'd gotten in too deep. Gray guessed the sheriff might be thinking the same thing.

"How does an intern get fired?" Sheriff Kruse asked.

"Gemma didn't want to let him go, but Clyde insisted on it. She'd seen Wes talking to Emil Atkins, the neighbor she suspects of harassing her and the tigers." Gray thought to ask the sheriff why he hadn't done more about that, but he needed the man on his side and didn't want to stir up trouble.

Sheriff Kruse stood, signaling their clandestine meeting was over. "I'll keep your cover, Gray. No need to worry about that. But in return I expect you to fill me in on anything that can help me solve this. I figure whoever is responsible for killing Wes is the same person behind the fire and also the attempts on Gemma's life. What I find interesting, though, is that each time she's been in trouble, you've been there to save her. The brakes, the rockslide and, last night, the fire."

Gray stood too. Interesting Sheriff Kruse knew about the rockslide. Had Gemma told him or someone else in the department? News traveled faster than one could imagine in rural areas.

"What do you make of that?" the sheriff finally asked.

Was the man accusing him of some crime?

"I suppose it was just great timing on my part. Someone up there is looking out for her."

"Are you sure it's not more than that?"

Maybe the sheriff wasn't accusing him so much as getting him to see things from a different perspective. And then he understood.

Sheriff Kruse nodded. He must have seen in Gray's eyes that he finally got it.

When the brakes went out, Gray had been there to save Gemma by happenstance, but the other times? He and Gemma had been together when someone had tried to kill her.

Kill *them*.

Someone wanted him dead too. Did someone know his true identity?

Three brutal days later, Gemma exited the shower at the end of many long hours of work, finally free from the dirt and grime and soot that came from not only her normal labor at Tiger Mountain but from cleaning up the scorched habitat.

At least the tigers were calming after the chaos the fire had caused. She dried off and got dressed, trying not to think about Caesar. The big, old cat had been caged and carted off this evening, after most of the volunteers and staffers had left for the day, including Gray who had promised to return later in his self-appointed role as her protector. But Ernie had stayed behind to help. He was the only one who knew. Clyde had asked him to stay and assist.

She'd wanted to share her displeasure with Clyde and perhaps get the chance to convince him they should move another tiger. But Clyde had left again, returning to Portland shortly before Caesar—groaning and distressed—had disappeared into the truck.

Gemma stayed with the cat, comforting and reassuring him the best she could, right until the doors of the truck were closed. Seeing him go had left her discouraged. And while Gemma would have preferred to leave Ernie with the impression it was for the best, instead huge tears had taken her hostage. Before she embarrassed herself, she offered up a lame excuse and hurried back to her cabin. The place had served to keep her close and in the middle of life on the sanctuary, but never before had it served as an escape. A hiding place.

What did other people do when everything in their lives seemed to be falling apart?

She definitely needed to talk to someone. Before, she would have turned to Clyde. But he had been so remote that she wasn't sure she even knew the man anymore. His years of experience traveling the world had put distance between them, not only physically but emotionally.

She saw that now.

Besides, how could she talk to him when she was so angry with him for arranging to move the tigers out without even a discussion? What gave him the right—well, besides the fact he was the money behind Tiger Mountain? Still, he'd left Gemma to manage the sanctuary.

Right. Look how great that was going.

Venting the only way she could at the moment, she grabbed a throw pillow and tossed it hard across the bedroom. Releasing some of the frustration helped, but she had a long way to go. Gemma moved to the kitchen and heated a bowl of soup in the microwave, but she wasn't hungry.

In the living room she dropped to the sofa and tugged on jogging shoes—the kind of shoes she could no longer use for their intended purpose since the accident—wanting to go for a good long walk. Alone. But that was too dangerous.

She couldn't run. She couldn't hike.

She couldn't even drive her CJ!

But that had nothing to do with danger. The vehicle had been totaled. Everything she loved was slowly being destroyed. Images of the damaged habitat accosted her mind. The fire had to be arson. Add the death of Wes into the mix and Gemma could barely think straight.

Why did life have to be so hard?

Guilt suffused her for the thought. *She* was alive. Wes hadn't fared so well.

What had happened? Had he gotten in the way of the arsonists who wanted Gemma dead? Why had he even been at Tiger Mountain?

Nausea swirled inside. Hugging herself, she stared out the window. It was still a couple of hours until night set in and the woods around the cabin would be dark. Was she safe? The sheriff mentioned she might think of leaving town for her own safety. His department simply wasn't staffed to provide a protection detail. But Gemma couldn't leave the tigers she'd devoted her life to. Besides, Gray insisted on continuing to watch over the sanctuary, and her, at night. He'd been there to save her life every time.

She stared out the window, remembering he'd instructed her to keep the curtains drawn.

The forest grew darker and, while she loved the view, she once again had the sense of someone watching her. Gemma reached for the drapes to close them, but her eyes caught on a figure moving in the shadows between the trees. She paused, staring out, searching the woods.

Someone was out there. Had they been watching her? Was it the person who wanted her dead?

She gulped for breath.

It was all the encouragement Gemma needed to leave.

Grabbing her cane and bag, she headed for the door and left the cabin, remembering to lock the door behind her. Of course, Gray's face came to mind as she remembered the night he'd scolded her about locking her door. The night he'd shown up to tell her about the brakes. She shoved thoughts of him away and hurried to the truck Tom left for her to use, which was parked beneath the carport. She hadn't gotten around to replacing the CJ with all that was going on. In her bag, she searched for the keys.

Why did she have to use such a big bag? She could swear she'd stuck the giant key ring with her copy of all the important keys in the side pocket. She resisted the urge to dump the contents out on the ground. Gemma glanced behind her to make sure she was still alone. Maybe she was overreacting again and someone had been out taking a walk. Even though everyone had gone home for the day, at least there was still some daylight left. Gemma drew a measure of comfort from that. Still, she didn't like the shadows lurking in the carport. But she'd never find the keys with her hands shaking like this.

Sucking in calming breaths, she steeled her mind against the panic. *You have to stop freaking out!*

And then jangling, the familiar feel of metal.

The keys!

Finally.

She gripped them in her sweaty palm to unlock the truck door. Her hand trembled and she struggled to get it right, the keys clanking, announcing to the quiet evening that Gemma was afraid of what lurked in the woods. When the key engaged the lock, and she opened the door, she climbed in and sighed with relief. Starting the ignition, she drove down the road out of the sanctuary.

The county road ended at Highway 101, which ran along the Oregon coast. If she headed south, she would hit Gold Beach, where the Rogue River emptied into the Pacific, in about twenty miles. Gemma headed north.

Then it started to rain and hard.

Again?

Turning on the windshield wipers, she glanced in the rearview mirror. Had another vehicle just turned out off the infrequently traveled county road? She couldn't be sure with the downpour, but that gray sedan remained behind her. She turned her attention to watching the road that hugged the coast.

Rain pelted the windshield, and she adjusted the windshield wipers to accommodate.

Where was the rain when the habitat was burning? They could have used it. As she drove the slick, curvy road, all the wrong that had happened swirled in a vortex in her head.

Her uncle Dave's voice came back to her from that night.

On this road.

In the rain.

Gemma, there's something I have to tell you. I've put it off much too long. It's about—what's happening? The brakes! I can't—I can't control it. I can't control the car. This is all my fault! He'd glanced over at her, horror and certainty in his eyes. *Gemma! I'm sorry... Gemma—*

The car had crashed into a tree, silencing him forever. Leaving Gemma alive but with a severely broken leg and nerve damage.

She sucked in a breath. The sheriff had ruled the wreck an accident. But Uncle Dave had been scared that night. He hadn't said as much, but she could hear it in his tone. Sense it. What if the wreck hadn't been an accident—what if it had been orchestrated by the same person who was now targeting her? She hadn't gotten around to asking Clyde about this possibility, but maybe she would the next time she saw him.

She continued on for a few more miles and noticed the same vehicle still following her. Could be nothing. But Gemma needed no other nudging to steer down the short drive to the house Gray had given for his address, realizing this had been her intended destination all along. She couldn't even trust herself to keep her distance. Despite her common sense, her resolve. Despite knowing she couldn't get involved with the guy and should avoid him. None of that made any difference. Her resolve was no match against her desire to see him.

Gray had a way of encouraging her, and Gemma had never been more desperate for it. Her positive nature had been decimated with the events of the last few weeks. Of course, tonight when she'd turned to lock her door, an image of Gray's face had come to mind. But if she was honest, he was never too far from her thoughts. She found herself thinking about him often. Her heart danced a little each day when he first showed up. And when she saw him leave for the day, the light seemed to fade, if only a little. Why was she thinking about him like this? She knew better.

She *knew* better. It would only end in heartache. Everyone had secrets and Gray certainly had his. She stopped in front of the cozy, cute house painted in light shades of blue and trimmed in white. Then she felt ridiculous. Nobody followed her down the drive. Had she imagined it? A sense of awkwardness settled over her. Was it rude of her to show up uninvited?

Oh, what am I doing here?

Gemma shifted into reverse. Maybe she could just drive away before he even noticed. Too late. Hands on his hips, he stood on the porch. His jacket on, he looked as if he'd been about to leave the house. Her heart did that thing. See, even the rain had stopped for him.

Okay. Shift already.

But no. She couldn't exactly leave now that he'd seen her and, in fact, stood there staring. Was he grinning? And oh…yeah, she needed Gray. What would he say if he knew how much she needed to be here right now?

Gray bounded down the porch steps and over to the truck door. He opened it. "Are you okay?" Deep concern filled his gaze.

"Yeah, I just…I just…" She couldn't bring herself to tell him about her complete paranoia. About seeing someone in the woods near her cabin and her fear she'd been followed. The gray sedan hadn't trailed her down this road.

"Well, don't just sit there. Get out and come in. We can sit on the porch and talk. It's a beautiful evening, especially since the rain stopped."

His kindness nearly undid her. Oh, good grief. She nodded and slipped out, forcing the sudden surge of tears back into the dungeon. She wanted to trust Gray, really wanted to trust him. The urge was frighteningly persistent. In fact, she had a feeling that she already trusted him but just didn't want to admit to what extent.

Once on his porch, he gestured at the wicker chairs with floral pads. He'd mentioned renting, so this obviously belonged to someone else. She couldn't see him picking this pattern out. But how would she know? She hadn't known him long enough to find out.

"I have lemonade, believe it or not. Or if you want something warm, how about hot chocolate or coffee?"

"No, thank you. Gray...I'm sorry for the intrusion. I—"

He sat next to her on the wicker sofa and took her hand. Her throat constricted.

"Something's bothering you. Tell me what happened."

Hanging her head, she shook it, feeling ridiculous for coming here. "Nothing's happened. It's not one thing. It's everything. And I needed someone to talk to."

He released her hand. "Why don't we take a stroll on the beach?"

He hadn't asked about her cane or if that would be a problem for her. He knew better by now. "I think I'd like that."

Taking her hand, he led her down the steps and the hundred yards to the beach. "What it must be like to have such a great view every day," she commented. "It's just beautiful here."

Gray shrugged. "It's okay. I prefer the views at Tiger Mountain though." He squeezed her hand.

Her heart flipped at his words. What had he meant by that? Or was she reading too much into it? She had to steer this walk and conversation to another place. But then the sun was setting, and Gray and Gemma stopped to watch. Sea stacks, rocky and beautiful, dotted the coast. Waves licked the shore at their feet, soothing her nerves.

"Nothing more amazing than the sunset on the Pacific." He released a breathy sigh.

Gemma wanted to be in his arms. But all she had was his hand. It was enough.

What am I doing? What am I thinking? I can't fall for this man, or any man.

She needed to talk to Gray about everything. That's why she was here.

"On the way here, I had a flashback. A memory of the night my uncle was killed."

Gray turned to look at her. "The accident that injured your leg?"

"Yes. I passed by the same exact spot today where his brakes went out and we slammed into a tree. It was raining that night too, so of course I would think of it."

He tugged her along with him and continued their walk. "Did you say the brakes went out?"

"I remembered tonight that he'd complained about the brakes right before the crash. But the officials said the vehicle hydroplaned. He lost control of the car. It was an accident."

Gray stopped and faced her. "Do you believe that?"

"I did at the time. I was young. Had just turned eighteen. I don't know what to believe now, but I remember I had a bad feeling about what he was going to tell me. I don't know—something about that night was weird. I was scared even before the car went off the road. My uncle had been afraid there would be an investigation because of accusations about abuse. Rumors. Lies. It was all lies, Gray. And here I am, going through this all over again in a manner of speaking. All I've ever wanted was to have my family back. The people I've loved but lost. I thought if I built a sanctuary for my parents and my uncle, maybe I could have some of what I lost back. I could rebuild their legacy as well as do my part in this world."

She glanced at him—saw the raw emotion there, the understanding—and then dropped her gaze to the waves rushing forward, chasing her feet. If she didn't step away, she'd get wet. It was the same with Gray. She was getting much too close to him. Why had she told him any of it? Why had she been this transparent and vulnerable? Or thought she should come here?

"I don't know why I'm telling you this. I don't even know you. Not really."

"Gemma." The way he said her name… She had to look up to him. His eyes reflected emotion. Compassion and something much more—it touched the deepest place in her heart. She hadn't known she wanted that from him, or needed it.

But could she let herself accept it?

No. She had to pull away.

TWELVE

"Gemma." Gray grabbed her arm, careful he didn't knock her off balance, but she seemed determined to leave him there. "Where are you going? Why are you so afraid to open up? I promise, I'm not going to hurt you."

She stared at him. Did she see the truth there—that he was hiding things from her and that he wouldn't allow himself to get close to her? Is that what had her scared to share with him like she'd just done? Her gaze, those hazel eyes of hers, laid him bare, revealing the truth he didn't want to admit—he couldn't make that kind of promise. And in her eyes, maybe that was answer enough, reason enough for her not to trust him.

When he'd made his resolution to never need anyone, he hadn't known he would meet Gemma Rollins. Hadn't known how she would affect him. But looking at her now, Gray thought he might just need this woman. Need Gemma.

He released her arm. Who was he to keep her when she clearly wanted to go?

Images washed over him—the engagement ring, Julia, the woman he wanted to marry kissing another. He couldn't allow himself to fall for anyone like that again. He stepped back, putting space between them but not enough. Not nearly enough when he was still fighting his urge to be closer to Gemma. Gray wanted to pull her to him and reassure her, wipe her fears and doubts away. Run his fingers through her long dark hair again.

He shut his eyes.

Whispered her name. Thought of that moment when he'd had his hands in her hair. Warmth suffused him. A wave rushed up near his feet, cold seawater splashing him, jarring him out of the trance she'd put him in.

No. Gray had to stay focused. Someone was trying to kill her. Someone was trying to kill them both. He'd been heading out to take up the night shift to watch over Tiger Mountain when he'd gotten a call from Sheriff Kruse. He wanted to meet Gray tonight, but he wouldn't say more on the phone. Then Gemma had driven up. She needed him right now and he had to focus on what was best for her, not what he wanted for himself. Besides, getting involved with her during this investigation was all kinds of wrong. His emotional involvement could cloud his judgment and ruin this investigation down the road, if anyone was charged.

She marched on ahead of him.

"Gemma, wait!" Gray caught up easily. "You're shivering. Come inside and have some hot chocolate."

As the setting sun ushered in dusk, Gray realized he didn't want her to return to her dark, lonely cabin.

Head lowered, Gemma kept walking.

"Come on, what do you say?"

She shrugged. "Yeah, sure. Okay."

He hadn't known her long, but he'd never seen her this down and it disturbed him more than it should. But she had every reason to struggle right now. Gray wasn't doing anything to help her. In fact, he was keeping a secret from her, as an undercover agent. If only he could tell her the truth.

Inside the house, he settled her on the sofa and made hot chocolate for them both. Gemma took the mug from him, her expression somber, her features pale. He understood all too well. Everything she cared about had been targeted. He wanted to question her further about the night her uncle died. His death could very well have been murder. Could he have been about to give her information about the trafficking ring that had been in operation for far too long? Was that why he had been killed? If it was murder and Clyde

Morris was responsible, how would Gemma react when she found out the truth? It would be devastating for her to learn that Clyde was behind it all. A man she held in high esteem.

He watched her sip on the drink a bit until the color came back into her cheeks. The silence wasn't deafening, like he might have expected, but comfortable. Two old friends sharing hot chocolate and listening to the waves crashing against the shore.

Gray broke the quiet with his words. "You're too hard on yourself, Gemma. You're always up, you stay positive and it's what draws people to you, but it's okay to be upset sometimes. It's okay to grieve." What was he? A therapist? But he was compelled to share what he could. "You're going through a lot right now, and if there's anything I can do to help, I will. I'm mostly concerned for your safety. Did the sheriff say anything to you? Did he suggest you get out of town for a while or at least stay with a friend instead of alone in your cabin?" This was Gray's way of making the suggestion, if the sheriff hadn't done that much. Gray watched over her cabin every night. Watched over the sanctuary. But standing watch hadn't been enough to stop the culprit so far and Gray still needed evidence to make an arrest.

"Yes, he made the suggestion. But I can't just up and leave Tiger Mountain. There's no one trained to take my place in the day-to-day management. And I guess I thought it was enough that you were watching the place at night." She sighed, then, "Thanks for that, by the way. I don't know how you do it all. And, thanks for listening, Gray. I guess I feel like I can talk to you. I've known Cara much longer, but I didn't want her to see me like this."

Despite her earlier reaction and doubts about revealing so much, talking to him when she really didn't know him, she apparently believed she could trust Gray enough to show him this side of herself. The real side.

He wasn't sure how he felt about that. "I understand. I'm here if you want to talk."

"Why is this happening?"

The question surprised him. He wasn't sure what she was asking, exactly. "What do you mean?"

She lifted her gaze. "Do you believe in God, Gray?"

Kind of sad she had to ask. That should be something easily seen in a person. "Of course I do."

"Well, I do too. For the longest time I've been hoping He would answer my prayers for the sanctuary. But He hasn't. Not as far as I can tell. So now instead of an answer to my prayers, I just want to know why all this is happening to me."

Wow. She was really unloading some deep stuff on him. He had to rub his jaw on that one. Boy, what did he say to that? Leaning back in the chair, he considered his words. *Lord, please help me to say the right thing.*

"I wish I had an answer for you. My brother committed suicide a few years ago, and I've always wondered the same thing. Why didn't God stop him? Why didn't He help *us* to stop Jeremy? To see how bad things had gotten. All I know is that we live in a fallen world and bad things happen. And maybe…maybe we can pray and God answers in ways we can't see and it doesn't all happen instantaneously. Maybe it's about the journey too."

She didn't respond, and he spent a minute worrying that he'd said the wrong thing. Maybe he should offer to pray with her? Or would that be insulting, implying that God was more likely to listen to him than to her?

"I wasn't expecting a real answer. Just expressing my thoughts. And why should I care so much about Tiger Mountain succeeding when someone is dead? Someone was murdered there. Someone tried to kill me too. And now Caesar is gone. Raja goes tomorrow."

"Wait. What?"

"Clyde wanted as few people to know as possible, but he's moving two tigers. He says we can't afford to keep all of them with the rebuilding expenses and the loss of space. He took Caesar this evening and I cried over that. I cried over a tiger when I should be more devastated over Wes. And I am. Maybe it's just the culmination of everything."

Pulse roaring in his ears at the news Clyde was moving Caesar, Gray struggled to listen to Gemma. Too much going on at once.

"Gray, are you listening?"

He rose, rubbing the back of his neck. He needed to make a call. "Yes, of course!"

He quickly sat right next to Gemma and grabbed her hands because he really did care about her, but moving the tigers could be the break in the case he'd been waiting on. "Where was Clyde taking the tigers? Why didn't I know about this?"

She tugged her hands free. "Why do you care so much? What's going on?"

He stood again and grabbed their cups. "Nothing. I'm just surprised I didn't know, that's all. I could have been there to help you. I'm sure it was hard. And I would've wanted to tell the old guy goodbye. Want some more hot chocolate?" Gray had overreacted at the news and had to play things down now.

Shaking her head, she said, "I've told you a lot about myself tonight, Gray. I don't know much about you. How about you reciprocate? Tell me something about you that I don't know, which is pretty much everything. I'd prefer to feel like this conversation isn't so one-sided."

"You know where I live." He grinned. And he did want to tell her everything. To be honest with her. She deserved it, but he was so close to ending this. Indecision tore through him.

When his cell rang, he glanced at the number. Mark, his superior. "Gemma, I have to take this call. And then… I'll tell you everything you want to know."

And maybe a few things she didn't.

Gray went out the front door and onto the porch to answer his call, leaving her alone.

This evening, Gray had been there for her once more. He's saved her again only this time it wasn't from physical harm as much as emotional angst. She'd been desperate or she never would have revealed so much of herself, but Gemma was glad she had shared. Gray had come through if only by listening. Was it so wrong to need someone who would listen and encourage you? She'd been that person for most everyone, and now she needed that too.

Except, with Gray, Gemma had to admit it went much deeper. Her heart had somehow gotten tangled up with him. Just being with him—walking or sitting, drinking hot chocolate or cleaning out a tiger habitat—made Gemma's heart lighter. She could almost wish he had never volunteered because she had been doing just fine before he showed up. Now on top of everything going on at Tiger Mountain, she had a thing for the guy right when a distraction was the last thing she needed.

And he was a stranger, to boot. Rising from the sofa, she peeked out the front window. Still on the phone and in a serious conversation by the tone in his voice. *I wonder who that is?* See, she didn't know enough about him to even make a guess.

Was it…was it his girlfriend? Did he already have a special woman in his life, the way that Ellis had? How would she know? While she didn't like to snoop, she had to know whom she could trust. She'd just spilled everything to this guy, even about the night Uncle Dave was killed.

That was it. She had to know if a secret fiancée was going to show up, if he was the man he claimed to be. Pacing around the small living room, she looked at the sparse decor of a rental home. Gray hadn't left anything personal.

Who are you, Gray Wilson?

She meandered around the small beachfront home to find the restroom and, next to that, a bedroom. The door was shut. Why shut the bedroom door in a house where you lived alone unless you wanted to keep out guests? Indecision pressed in on her. Should she open it or not? Moisture slicked her palms, but determination drove her forward. Gemma had to know who Gray was. She grabbed the doorknob and twisted.

Inside the room, his things were scattered. A duffel bag crumpled on the floor in the corner. Shirts and jeans were spread out on the bed as if recently laundered but not yet put away. He hadn't expected company, that was for sure. Listening to him around the corner, she could tell he was still deep in the conversation, but that could end any minute.

She'd come to him, desperately needing his knack for reassurance, and now she would repay him by snooping. Another desperate need—to know the truth. Ellis had been hiding something, and she couldn't let herself go any deeper with Gray, a man she'd only just met, when there was still so much she didn't know about him. It wasn't like she had to go digging through his things. Everything was laid out for her to see on the small desk against the wall. A laptop was open but in sleep mode. A stack of papers and a thick file. His wallet.

And a gun.

Not so unusual out in the wilderness, but, still, seeing it made her nervous.

Next to the desk, a black leather briefcase. Slowly, she flipped his wallet open and there she found a badge and ID. US Fish and Wildlife Service Special Agent? What was that? The FBI of game wardens?

Special Agent Grayson Wilde.

Gemma dropped the badge, stunned at the discovery.

A federal agent working at Tiger Mountain under a false identity? She pressed her hands to her lips. What was going on?

And he'd lied to her. Kept this all to himself. He was obviously working undercover.

Pain scorched her heart. Right. She'd known not to trust or care for anyone. She'd been through this before. Maybe she hadn't discovered a hidden fiancée, which he could still very well have, but she had learned he was lying about everything else. Lying about the reason he was at Tiger Mountain and about his true identity.

Gemma let fury boil up and compel her forward.

She had to get out of here.

But she didn't want to exit through the front door where he would see her and try to stop her. There had to be a back door in the place and she could sneak around the house to her truck before he saw her. She found it through the kitchen and carefully hurried down the steps hidden in the shadows. Darkness had settled in for the night, except for the light from a crescent moon now that the clouds had moved out again. Gemma made her way around the house, spotting the truck sitting only a few yards away. On this side of the house, moonlight guided her way.

Pain ached up her leg, the nerve endings firing off, slowing her efforts. Making her clumsy. So weird how the pain was connected to her emotions this way.

"Gemma!" Gray called from the porch. "Gemma, wait."

Footfalls approached behind her. If only she could reach the truck before he got to her. Climb in and drive off before she had to face him. She hadn't wanted to admit just how much she needed Gray, needed to trust him, but the depth of the pain in her heart proved it.

Her cane wobbled to the right, the pain in her leg causing her to crumple. Sparkling sand came at her as she fell, but strong arms swooped her up and in against Gray. *No, please no, not again.*

"Let me go!" She twisted away and he gently released her.

"What's wrong, Gemma?"

Now that she had her balance back, she continued to her truck and opened the door. No thanks to Gray—it was because of him her balance had been off in the first place.

He held the door, so she couldn't shut it. "Are

you going to tell me what's going on? Why you're so angry?"

He wouldn't let her go? Fine, they'd just have to get the confrontation out of the way right now. "I don't appreciate being lied to, that's what. I want to know the truth, Gray *Wilde*. Why are you at Tiger Mountain?"

THIRTEEN

Gray had done this to her.

He was the one to put those huge tears in her eyes, pouring over and sliding down her soft cheeks. He'd never thought he'd be so vulnerable to a woman's tears, but he could hardly stand to watch. They weren't tears of sadness or of grief. No. Gemma had now found herself again. She was the strong woman he'd met that first day. Anger blazed in her eyes instead.

She held up a fist and he knew she wanted to hit him. But she held back the fury carving lines through her beautiful face and then dropped her fist. "You lied to me!"

He said nothing because it was true. That's what one did when working undercover. But there was one thing he could say.

"Thank you."

"For what?" she snapped.

"For not hitting me."

"You don't think you deserve it?"

Maybe he did, and he hesitated before he answered. She couldn't understand what he'd gone through, growing close to her and keeping this to himself.

"I hope you realize that I have to tell Clyde. He's my main investor and the support behind this whole endeavor. He needs to know we're under investigation."

If Clyde Morris found out about his investigation, it could ruin everything. Not only would it put the investigation at risk, but it might actually make Clyde lash out at Gemma. He had to tell her everything and convince her to stay quiet, at least for now.

His feelings, her feelings—it all had to take a backseat to the investigation.

"No. You can't tell anyone. It's for your own safety. Do you understand?"

"I won't understand until you tell me everything, and this time, I want the truth. Who are you, really? Why are you at Tiger Mountain?"

"I wanted to tell you. In fact, before the call, I was about to tell you who I am."

"Right."

She tried to tug the door shut, but Gray remained where he stood. In her way. He couldn't let her run off until they had an understanding.

"Now that you know, we need to talk. I need you to listen. Can you please step out of the truck and come inside?" He hadn't meant his tone to sound so forceful and cold, but he had to get a handle on this before all was lost.

Fear shone in her eyes, hitting him like a fist to the gut. When he spoke again, he was careful to soften his tone.

"Gemma, you know me. You know the real me. Whoever I am, you know me as a person. I'm the same Gray that you've come to know and work with at Tiger Mountain. It's just my job that you didn't know about. Please give me the chance to explain. I'm here to help you, and I have been ever since I found you stranded in the Jeep."

Would his earnest words spoken in a gentle tone be enough to convince her to come inside? She blew out a breath. Hung her head back and looked at the stars, in obvious indecision. The tears streaking her face almost had a fluorescent glow about them in the moonlight. When she dropped her gaze to him, he saw the deep pain there as her eyes searched his.

He couldn't help himself. He wiped away a tear with his thumb, brushing the soft skin of her cheek. She shuddered. Was that from his touch? He was getting in too deep, much too deep. He pulled away. "Well?"

"How can I believe anything you say?"

"How about I share my story and then you can decide?"

Frowning, she averted her gaze. "How can I argue with that?"

She couldn't. "Then come inside and I'll tell you everything. Answer all your questions."

She frowned, considering…and then nodded.

He slowly released a breath and relaxed his shoulders. At least he'd convinced her to give him more time to explain. But, in the meantime, a tiger was getting away. Gray needed to protect Gemma and also find Caesar. If it was too late to get him, then Gray would have to be on hand when Raja was taken away, tomorrow. He knew enough now that he could be on top of it when it happened. But for everything to work as planned, he needed Gemma's silence.

Once inside the house, Gemma settled in the same place he'd left her before her mad escape.

"How did you find out?"

Her eyes widened. "You left your ID and badge on the desk in your room."

"And you were in my room why?" Now it was his turn to be furious, and not just at Gemma but at himself. How could he be so stupid? But he couldn't think straight when he was with her.

Her gaze darted around the room as she looked at anything but Gray. "With everything that's happened, I needed to know who I could trust. I needed to know for sure. I wanted to trust you, to believe in you—can't you see that? But you were so secretive, even after I told you my story. I wanted to find out what you were hiding."

"And now you know."

"Not really. It's not making sense to me yet. You are stalling. Tell me everything, Gray."

"The reason I'm working undercover is because I received a tip that someone involved with Tiger Mountain is also involved in a wildlife trafficking ring. They planned to use your sanctuary to traffic tigers, specifically tiger body parts. And now, it sounds like that is actually happening."

She gasped. "You can't be serious. How is that possible? Who would do such a thing?"

"Gemma, please tell me you're not involved."

She stood then, stunned at his suggestion. He held his hands up in surrender. "I don't believe you are. I just had to ask."

"No, you didn't have to ask. Are you investigating me? Do you know what an investigation will do to us if the public finds out? Rumors of animal abuse killed our funding before. Without funding, yeah, it's hard to take care of animals. Clyde expects me to raise my own donor base, which I won't be able to do if we're under investigation. I can't believe this. I thought I could build something new. It's like I can never escape the past. This is like what happened before."

"Yes, it is, and who was involved then besides your now deceased family members?"

Those tears again, surging in her eyes, but she

didn't allow them to overflow their boundaries. Gray hated doing this to her. Wanted to pull her into his arms as if that could make everything go away.

Her gaze held his. She didn't say the words, but he could see the moment she realized the truth.

Clyde Morris. He'd been the one all along.

"I…how could I not have seen? How could I not know?"

He'd asked the same questions when he first arrived, but then he saw how Clyde operated, leaving Gemma to the day-to-day running of the sanctuary. This sanctuary was only one small piece of Clyde's extensive trafficking operation. Looked like Clyde was happy to let Gemma have her sanctuary as long as he could use it for his own purposes. He'd been much more than a silent partner.

And Gemma had fallen in love with the tigers and gotten in the way.

"I can't believe Clyde would try to kill me, though. Gray, no, this can't be the truth. Please, there has to be someone else. Besides, *why* would he try to kill me? He needs me to run the sanctuary."

More questions without answers. He ached for her. Her expression shifted to one of terror. Horror even. "Caesar!"

Grimly, he nodded. "Yes, Caesar. While we sit here and talk, Caesar is likely being taken to slaughter." To be divided into parts and sold to the highest bidder in the traditional Asian medicine market. But he kept that to himself.

She jumped to her feet. "We have to stop it. We have to save Caesar."

He grabbed her shoulders. "Whoa. There's no 'we' about this. I'm the government operative with the training to deal with this. You need to stay out of it. You've faced too much danger already. Let me do my job, and maybe I can save Caesar."

"Wait a minute." She pressed a finger to her lips. "I might be able to help. The company that took him away—we've worked with that specific trucking company before. I can search the files on the computer. See if I can find something about their base of operations that you can use or maybe their delivery destination. Find out where they might take Caesar."

He shook his head. "That would be too dangerous, Gemma."

"I'm already in danger. Someone has already tried to kill me. But nobody will suspect me of doing something secretive on the office computer. You, however, someone would suspect."

"You said Clyde had gone to Portland. When is he due back?"

"Tomorrow. So there's time. We can do this."

"Are you sure?" He paced again. "And, then,

what about tomorrow and the day after that? I'm not sure how long you can keep up this ruse without letting on that you know." He rubbed his eyes, wishing Gemma could come up with an excuse to leave town, but she was integral to Tiger Mountain, especially in their current predicament.

"Then we have to finish this. You have to find the evidence you need before it's too late."

He nodded. "Tonight then. See what you can find on the computer tonight. I'll catch up with you at the office. I need to make some calls and see if we can find out where Caesar is going from my end. Let my superior know what is going on. Get a hold of Sheriff Kruse. This is happening and soon." He couldn't help the hope that rose at the very real possibility he would find the evidence to bring Clyde Morris and his trafficking ring down.

But something troubled him, dousing his momentary rush. Gemma was selfless and might have been thinking about Caesar, but Gray was thinking about her. He had to finish this before she got hurt. Gemma's life was still in danger.

"Gemma, this is dangerous. You understand that, right?"

"I've been in danger since the day we met, Gray. Nothing has changed except that now I know the truth and I can protect myself." She hesitated.

"What?"

"I didn't tell you this before. I saw someone in the woods near my cabin tonight. I was afraid they were watching me so I got in the truck. And then I thought someone followed me. That's when I came to your house."

"Why didn't you tell me?"

"I don't know if I'm being paranoid or not."

"You have every reason to be cautious. That does it. I can't let you go back there tonight."

But Gray had let her return to the sanctuary. That's because Gemma had come up with the bright idea to hang out with Cara. Clyde was in Portland, as it was, so having Cara with her at all times seemed like overkill. Still, Gray had cautioned she couldn't be too careful. He was meeting with the sheriff and then would catch up with her here.

In the meantime, Gemma didn't know what she would do without Cara. Her friend had agreed to hang out with her this evening while Gemma worked. She'd given the true excuse that she was afraid to be alone with everything that had been going on. Cara had gone so far as to invite Gemma to stay with her and her husband until she was out of danger and things settled down.

She was feeling a lot better, and her positivity was beginning to return. But she wouldn't put

Cara in any further danger and kept the details to herself.

"I haven't seen that in a while, you know?" Cara leaned against the doorjamb.

"What's that?" But Gemma had a feeling she knew.

"Your smile."

"It's not a real smile. I can't really smile until this is over."

"I hear you. I'm making a pot of coffee. You want some?"

She shook her head. "That would keep me up all night. On second thought, yes."

Gemma booted up the new desktop in the back office that Clyde had taken over while he was here. He mentioned leaving the machine behind for general use once he was done. A new computer, compliments of Clyde. She could replace the older one in her office with the latest model. She really was beholden to him, which made her snooping around in the files feel wrong. Surely there was some mistake. Clyde couldn't be the one behind the trafficking ring. And even if he was, why would he put anything on this machine that could be remotely incriminating? He knew she had access to it. He'd given her the password to log on, when Cara was busy in her office, in-putting the data on each tiger. Another thing that had been bothering her: if Clyde was the man who wanted her dead, then who had she seen in the woods? Who had followed her? Maybe she really was being paranoid and it was nothing to be worried about.

Leaning her chin forward against her hand, she huffed.

What am I doing? Clyde can't be involved. He simply can't be. Regardless, she'd assured Gray she wouldn't reveal his identity to Clyde. She'd been here before. Someone else long ago had begged her not to tell the truth. To keep his secret hidden. She shoved the thoughts away. This was completely different.

Believing that Clyde was innocent gave her a new resolve. She would prove he wasn't part of a trafficking ring. To that end, she would search through the files, starting with information about the trucking company that had transported Caesar today, to see if she could find out where they might have taken him. She could even put in a call about the delivery.

The prospect of finally getting some answers was exciting. Now she understood Gray better. Solving a mystery and catching bad guys might even be addictive.

The truck that had taken Caesar was with Beacon Transport. She found the file, a trucking company specializing in wild animal transportation, no less. She was familiar with the company to a point, but they hadn't needed animals transported very often. Once tigers arrived, they rarely left until they died. That was the way a sanctuary was supposed to be—their home for life. That's why the idea of trafficking animals via a sanctuary didn't make sense to her, but, in that way, perhaps it was the perfect cover. And the fire had conveniently necessitated the moving of tigers.

The company was scheduled to transport Caesar to another sanctuary in Colorado, so the information said, but, oddly enough, the payment didn't match up with the cost of travel to Colorado. Looked like they were only getting paid to haul Caesar a short distance.

Her heart stumbled.

Gemma frowned. Finding a pad of paper, she searched for a pencil to write down the information. There weren't any on the desk and when she tried a drawer, it was locked. Why lock a desk drawer unless there was something to hide? If she broke into the drawer, she would actually be snooping on something Clyde believed important enough to lock. But he shouldn't hide anything from Gemma regarding Tiger Mountain. Using a paper clip, she picked the lock easily enough. So much for security.

Gray should be on his way by now. She wished he would hurry up.

Inside the drawer was a bill of lading regarding the transportation of two tigers to…a…warehouse? So Clyde *was* involved. The hurt she felt over his duplicity blurred her vision.

Voices resounded in the hall.

Not Gray.

Gemma froze.

Clyde.

How could that be?

He was supposed to be in Portland!

Gemma shoved the drawer closed and looked at the computer screen, pulling up a blank document. Pulse pounding, she started typing out a letter to whomever it may concern.

Clyde meandered into the office. "Gemma! What a surprise to see you here."

Cara appeared in the doorway behind him. "Hey Gem, I'm going to head on out now. Ted burned the lasagna. Now that Clyde is here, you don't have to worry about being on your own."

Gemma nodded. What could she say to keep her friend here with Clyde looking on? "Okay. Enjoy your dinner."

Glancing up at him, she couldn't even rouse a smile. "I thought you were still in Portland raising money?"

He slid onto the edge of the desk and studied her. With him looming over her like that, she'd never felt so uncomfortable under his scrutiny.

But then, had she ever been under his scrutiny like this?

"Are you okay, Gemma?"

Could he smell fear?

No, I'm not okay! She'd thought of this man as a father, especially since losing her parents and then her uncle. Even from a distance, he'd filled that place for her as though he'd wanted to. Calling to check on her now and then. As though she truly mattered to him. But had he simply been using her? "I'm fine, Clyde. Still missing Caesar, that's all." She rubbed her face, revealing how tired she truly was, trying to act completely normal. "So what's up? Why'd you come back early?"

"I finished my business. With the fire and the recent problems, the funding isn't exactly flowing in like it should. I ended up talking to the sheriff tonight. You'll be glad to hear that he believes Wes might have been behind the attempts on your life and the other troubles."

She didn't see it. "Why would he do that?"

"While you were busy putting out the proverbial and literal fires, he could transport a tiger or two. But obviously things got out of hand. Didn't go as he planned."

"Why try to kill me?" And who had killed Wes? But she didn't say it out loud. She didn't want an actual conversation with Clyde and had already asked too many questions. The sooner he left, the better.

"Because you didn't make it easy for him to grab one of the cats, the way that he wanted. You were too close. At any hint of a disturbance, you left your cabin to check on the tigers. But with you out of the way, he might have had a chance. His sister is dying, and he needed the money."

She focused on the screen, typing her fake letter, wondering if Gray had known about Wes's sister.

"Why do you say that?"

"What?" She glanced at him.

"Why did you ask if Gray knew about Wes?"

Oh no. Had she said that out loud? Heart pounding, she scrambled for an answer. "Gray has taken it upon himself to protect me."

"He's done a lousy job, if you ask me."

Well, she hadn't asked him. And she was still alive thanks to Gray, so there. Gemma filed the document away and then shut down the computer. "Look, Clyde, I'll admit that I kind of like him. I don't mind him being around so much even if I no longer need protection." With that, Gemma was able to find a reason to smile, and it had the unexpected effect of putting Clyde off.

He didn't even crack a grin.

He was giving off strange vibes. Was she acting suspiciously? Did he realize she'd figured him out? He'd practically caught her snooping in his office. She'd never been more terrified. It was like she was seeing him for the first time. Who was this man?

Could Clyde see in her eyes what chilled her to the marrow?

Gemma was afraid for her life.

FOURTEEN

Clyde angled his head as if considering what to say. He obviously hadn't expected to find her in here like this after hours. And in his eyes, she saw what she dreaded.

He suspected she'd learned the truth about him.

She had to act as though nothing was out of the ordinary. Get out of here before it was too late. Stay calm. Just stay calm. "Well, I'm tired. It's been a long day and I need to head home." Gemma eased out of the chair and struggled to steady her breathing.

Could he hear her heart pounding in cadence with her rising panic? Where was Gray? He was supposed to be here by now.

The man she once thought was like family to her said nothing. He simply watched her as she walked out the door and headed down the hallway. She knew what he would do next. He would open his computer and try to see what she'd been up to—what files she had accessed.

Then he would search his desk drawer and find it unlocked. She had a few seconds to escape. If only her leg didn't ache with her stress, adding to an already precarious situation. With the pain, her leg stiffened and it was like walking with a leg in a cast.

Heart pounding to get free of her chest, she pushed through the front door.

Run!

But she couldn't run; she could only hobble along. She had no intention of going back to her cabin. No. She would leave in the truck and meet Gray. But once she was at the vehicle, she realized she'd left the keys sitting on the desk in Clyde's office. Idiot! It had been all she could do to grab her cane and leave. She was doing the worst job of pretending everything was all right.

No way could she go inside and face Clyde.

Feeling her disability like never before, she carefully made her way through the woods in between the resource building and her cabin and tried to keep hidden as she headed for the road. Tugging her cell from her pocket, she tried to reach Gray to warn him and ask him to hurry.

She was in trouble!

But she couldn't get a signal here. Gemma pushed on, hugging the edge of the woods, heading away from the sanctuary. She had loved living here. Loved the hope that ignited in her heart that she could once again create something of what she knew growing up, create a legacy for the family that she'd lost. But she couldn't have been more wrong.

Exhausted, Gemma paused and looked at her phone. Finding a signal at last, she called Gray again.

He answered. She never thought his voice could sound so good.

"Where are you?" she practically screamed through the phone.

"What's wrong?"

"Come and get me now. I'll be hiking down the road to the main highway. Please hurry."

"I'm on my way already. Tell me what's happened."

"It's Clyde. He walked in on me on the computer. He didn't say anything, but by the look in his eyes, he suspects I know. And Cara thought I'd be fine with him there, so she left."

"What?"

"She didn't know I was afraid of Clyde. She thought when he got there she could leave." Clyde wouldn't have done anything in front of Cara unless he suspected she knew something too. Instead, she'd made it clear she was oblivious.

"Okay, stay hidden. I'll be right there. I've been on the phone with my superior. I was just with the sheriff. The medical examiner said the chemical etorphine had killed Wes."

His tone sounded almost accusing.

"What?" Oh, that made her sick. That tranquilizer was meant for big animals like elephants and rhinos. It wasn't legal for her to use it at the sanctuary. And it would have killed Wes instantly. "That's not what we use in our tranquilizer guns. We use ketamine."

"I know who used it, Gemma. It's a prominent tranquilizer among wildlife traffickers. And as soon as Sheriff Kruse said Clyde had stopped in to speak with him tonight, I tried to call your cell and warn you."

"I had trouble even getting this signal."

"The sheriff was headed over to see Emil Atkins to question him about Wes and the fire. Clyde has really done a number on him, but then he got called to an emergency. I'll call 911, but it will take a deputy time to get there. I'm on my way. And, Gemma?"

"Yes?"

"Stay alive."

"I promise I'll do my best. What are you going to tell the emergency dispatcher? You don't have any evidence to arrest Clyde yet, Gray. This will ruin your investigation. And Clyde will run after tonight. I'm sure of it. My life will always be in danger."

"I'll tell them you're afraid for your life. You're more important to me than this investigation. I'm only a few minutes—"

"Gray?" She glanced at the phone.

She'd lost the signal.

Please, God, if you answer one prayer, please answer this one. Help me get to safety. Help Gray make it in time.

But doubt suffused her. She'd already been through so much and where had God been? Where was He now?

Her cane and stiff leg hampered her efforts to put distance between her and Clyde, and the terrain at night made her travel all the more difficult. All the hurdles life had thrown her had now been reduced to tangled and gnarled tree roots, boulders and rocks and slippery moss—the smallest of hindrances seemed insurmountable to her.

"Gemma!" Clyde's voice echoed through the dark woods—the forest she loved had now turned menacing.

No, no, no. He can't find me. Come on, Gray!

That Clyde would use the sanctuary for his own trafficking purposes—a man who claimed he made wildlife conservation his mission in life—seemed surreal to her. But she'd seen the evidence herself. If only she had thought to grab the documentation. But there had not been time. He'd shown up, appearing out of nowhere, as if he knew she'd discovered the truth. How could she have been so blind?

She had no more doubts that Clyde was involved in illegal trafficking, using Tiger Mountain—the words screamed through her head. He'd been more than exuberant when she'd come to him four years ago with her request for his help in building a new sanctuary.

Now she suspected that the night Uncle Dave died, he had been going to tell her the truth about Clyde. Gray had implied that the trafficking ring went back that far. An awful question suddenly occurred to her—if Uncle Dave really had been planning to tell her about Clyde, was it a truth he himself had discovered? Or had he been working with Clyde? She couldn't know.

Had Gray called 911? Where was he? What was taking so long?

Clyde called after her again. "Gemma, what are you doing? Where did you go? Are you hurt?"

He sounded so normal, just the way he always had. He was trying to make her think she was crazy, and that everything was all right. That he wasn't a killer. She wasn't about to listen. Twigs scraped her face as she hurried.

A protruding root caught her foot and she fell forward with a jar, stifling a cry. She'd never make it down the road at this rate. Gemma would have to hide in the sanctuary itself, until Gray or the sheriff arrived to help her. But what would happen once they came? Until Clyde physically harmed her, it would only look like she had lost her mind. Clyde would find an angle to spin everything against her, especially given he'd gone out of his way to speak with the sheriff tonight already. She realized now that he had manipulated everything and had the situation well under control.

God, please no. Please, help me to bring him down. He'd gotten away with too much for far too long. And Gemma had been stupid and naive.

A drop pelted her. And then another.

Of course. Of course it would rain now, making the slow-going even more slow and miserable. Still, that could help her, making it more difficult for Clyde to spot her. But it could also hurt her. She had to hide and stay hidden.

The only place she could think to hide was within the sanctuary itself. That could buy her some time, especially since she knew the space much better than Clyde did. Before the rain came down too hard, before her cell died completely, she texted Gray her plans to hide and wait Clyde out. When she got a signal, the text would go through.

"I know you're in the woods. You know with your leg that you can't get away from me." His call echoed through the gloomy forest. "Don't make me look for you. Come out and I promise I won't hurt you. Come on, Gemma. I'm practically family."

A deep, throbbing ache coursed through her at his words. He'd as much as admitted he was guilty. *Family?* she cried out on the inside. *You killed my family!* She had no evidence of this, but she knew in her heart that it was true. And if she got away, she would find the proof. The truth had to come out.

What about Wes? Did you kill him? Did you tell him those words? she wanted to cry out. *What about Caesar and Raja?* But calling out would only give away her location.

But it didn't matter. Clyde's voice revealed he was heading in her general direction.

He was close, entirely too close.

Gray slowly steered his Silverado down the county road that cut through the sanctuary, windshield wipers squeaking back and forth as he searched for Gemma, hoping she would step out into his headlights when she realized it was him. The beams of his lights would only go so far, and outside of that circle of light, darkness loomed in the woods, making it all but impossible for him to see anything. Tree branches stretched out across the road, shadows turning them into ghoulish arms reaching for frightened trespassers.

She had to be terrified out there alone in the dark with Clyde possibly onto her. Gray silently berated himself. He should have anticipated the man wouldn't have gone so far as Portland when a tiger was being moved. He probably lied to Gemma about his travel plans so he could conduct his trafficking transaction without drawing attention.

Where are you, Gemma?

She was expecting him and was supposed to wait in the woods. But he'd already made it to the resource building and hadn't seen Gemma.

Why hadn't she taken Tom's truck out? Clyde must have somehow prevented her. Where was the man? Gray checked the cell again and found a text from Gemma.

I'm hiding in the sanctuary.

Clyde was obviously stalking her. How long could she hope to elude him? Maybe the habitats would assist her in staying hidden. Gray texted her, hoping it wouldn't come through at an inappropriate moment.

I'm here. Where are you exactly?

He didn't wait for a response. Donned his jacket, made sure his Glock was in his shoulder holster and his extra pistol in his ankle holster. He never removed the small knife hidden in his belt. Confirming no one lurked in the shadows around his truck, he got out and headed toward the habitats. Clyde would have seen Gray's vehicle approach. Gray wouldn't go in through the front gates of the fenced-in portion, where Gemma was hiding. That would be too obvious and Clyde could be monitoring the gate and then take Gray out.

He'd have to walk the perimeter and climb over—not a little daunting. Regardless, it had to be done fast. Clyde could already have found Gemma and hurt her, or worse, killed her. Panic and fear for her urged him through the shadows, between the trees and over to the fence, though he remained in darkness.

Where was the sheriff's department when you needed them?

At least the rain had eased up into a fine mist. He hurried until he was a least five hundred yards from the resource building and against the outer fence. Then he'd have another fence to conquer—all part of the protective measures to keep the tigers in place. Now to breach the split-rail fencing and keep the chain-link from rattling so he wouldn't broadcast his location to Clyde. That meant Gray had to ascend both quietly and quickly.

Near the top he slipped, catching himself before he plummeted to the ground but not without making an entire section of fence clang. He stilled, holding his breath as if that could make him look like one of the rails between sections. On this dreary night, anything was possible.

Finally he made his way over the top, which included another section tilted at a forty-five degree angle to make things even more complicated. He climbed down until it was comfortable to simply drop to the ground. Immediately, he began to jog between the interior and exterior fencing, seeking another entry point. He'd made too much noise back there, even with the rain to cover the sound.

He scaled the next fence and just before he released his hold on the fence he hesitated. Movement in his peripheral vision caught his attention.

Gray froze and watched.

Something moved near a thicket of trees. Something large and…catlike.

Great. Had someone let a tiger out? Had it been Gemma or Clyde? Was she even in the sanctuary anymore? Gray dropped to the ground with a thud, again making more noise than he would have liked. He remained still, waiting and watching for any signs of Clyde, Gemma or tigers. Then he quietly rushed to the side of a building. Without knowing where she'd hidden, finding Gemma could take a while. At least most of the acreage was fenced in to contain each tiger. He wouldn't be looking there. Not yet.

Squeezing his eyes shut, he tried to picture her and imagine where she might hide from Clyde. A place that he also wouldn't guess.

Obviously, Clyde realized his game was up and the father figure had now turned dangerous and deadly. He wouldn't let anything interfere with his operation, which was worth millions and which provided him with a niche in which he'd thrived for decades.

Gray could almost be happy that the noose was tightening around Clyde's neck, except he didn't want anyone else to die because of the trafficking ring. And this time he might lose a woman he cared deeply about. Even if she'd never forgive him for lying about his reasons for coming to Tiger Mountain.

Trust, once lost, was hard to regain. He'd seen that well enough with the tigers, especially with Raja who'd been blindsided and now no longer trusted Gemma.

Gray peered around the building and saw not one but two tigers prowling through the thicket. Tigers were normally solitary creatures. These could be the sisters, Layla and Lilly.

Great, just great.

Tigers were generally stealth hunters, but given that these animals had been abused before coming to Tiger Mountain, he wasn't exactly sure what he could expect with them. Would he become their prey? Or a toy to be played with?

A security light illuminated a habitat building about fifty yards from him, and next to a tree Gray spotted someone. Though it was too far and too dark to see clearly, he could at least see the person was taller and thicker than Gemma.

Clyde.

His gut churning, Gray searched his immediate area and then backtracked around the building. Maybe he could come up behind the man and stop him. Glancing through the fence and trees and toward the county road, he wished he would see headlights approaching or hear sirens. Something. Looked like the cavalry wasn't coming. One thing he was certain of: he couldn't *do* this alone. Too many dangers were converging at one place and time. Too much could go wrong.

God, I know You're always with me, but tonight I'm going to need Your help in a big way. Maybe tonight can be the night You answer some of Gemma's prayers. She believes. She hasn't lost faith or turned away from You. She's waiting on You.

And I'm waiting on You too.

He needed to get evidence and arrest Clyde, but all he could think about was Gemma. Her hazel eyes that could pierce right through his soul and search him out. He had a feeling that she'd known all along he was hiding something. He wished he hadn't kept things from her. If he'd been honest sooner, maybe they could have avoided this predicament with Clyde. Gray couldn't let her get hurt physically or otherwise.

Please, God!

She'd already been through so much, and he couldn't help but admire her strength in the face of great obstacles. Her determination to make a home for abused tigers, something that was bigger than herself. Bigger than one person.

Her passion to make a difference in the world.

God had charged mankind, beginning with Adam, with caring for the garden and the animals. Gray didn't think anything about that task had changed. Sure, people needed to love one another, but they also needed to care for and be responsible for the earth and God's creatures. All Gemma wanted was to do good work—and yet all of this tragedy had fallen on her head.

Gray edged to the corner of the building and gulped a breath. He peered around the corner.

Clyde was gone. And no Gemma either.

And right now God, I have to save one of Your creatures. Help me to do it. Help me to find her.

FIFTEEN

Cold chilled her to the bone. The kind that crawled under her skin to stay when she'd been out in the elements too long. Her rain-soaked clothes didn't help. Pressing deeper into the shadows between the trees, Gemma hugged herself and shivered.

All she could think about was finding some place warm and dry.

Where was Gray?

He should be here by now. Had he arrived without her noticing? She hadn't been able to keep an eye on the road. At first, she'd thought to hide in one of the buildings, but she'd left the key ring behind—the same key ring with the truck key. She decided hiding in one of the cat buildings would disturb the tigers too much, anyway, and she couldn't risk drawing attention. Then she thought back to the night someone had locked her and Gray inside and started a fire. She wouldn't put herself in that position again.

And now, Clyde had released a few of the tigers. Lured them outside with meat and completely opened up their fenced-off spaces, leaving them to roam outside of their own habitats. He had effectively turned the sanctuary into the danger zone.

What was the man trying to do? Kill them all? He could just as easily be mauled by a tiger.

Then she spotted Clyde. He stood beneath a tree near the trunk. A security light illuminated his form, and she could just make out his weapon. From here, she couldn't tell if it was a dart gun or a real gun. He shifted in the light. Wait…it was bigger than their dart guns.

He carried a large pistol.

Her breath caught. Since when did he carry a gun? She felt like she didn't even know him. Had she ever? How could she trust another human being if even the man who had been a close family friend betrayed her like this? Had he also betrayed her parents? Her uncle? She tasted the bile in her throat.

What was it with people who pretended to be someone else?

Remaining in the shadows so he wouldn't see her, she could only hope—and yes, pray—one of the tigers didn't sniff her out and reveal her presence to the man with the gun.

Gray, where are you?

Where would he think I would go to hide? Her cell had long ago died, so she couldn't text her location. With Clyde effectively flushing her out by opening up habitats and luring tigers out, she couldn't stay hidden much longer.

A raucous noise drew her attention. Through the trees she could see Layla and Lilly fighting over the hunk of meat Clyde had thrown in their direction. Gemma glanced back at the tree. Clyde was no longer there. She searched the buildings and bushes, habitats and the shadows, but she couldn't see Clyde. Behind her, mud squished.

Her heart jumped up her throat. Panic engulfed her. Had Clyde found her? Though adrenaline pumped through her veins, Gemma was afraid to respond to her body's need to fight or run. When she could no longer stand it, she prepared to launch from the tree and spring—or hobble with her cane. But just before she shoved off, another possibility hit her.

Maybe it wasn't Clyde but instead was a tiger. They stalked their prey, getting close as possible before they pounced. She didn't want to believe that they would pounce on *her*, though. These were her tigers—not pets, no, but she had a relationship with them. She loved them. Gave them the space they deserved as God's creatures, food and shelter. Took care of them until she was too tired to move at the end of the day. In turn, they seemed to know her. Like her. Appreciate her. But they were still inherently wild all the same, and hadn't she brought them to Tiger Mountain so they could revert to their natural instinctive behaviors? They were innocent animals caught up in this and once again used for selfish purposes—something from which she'd tried, and failed, to save them. If she ran now, maybe a tiger would chase her down. But she wouldn't let Clyde catch her.

She wouldn't give him the satisfaction.

Except all her resolve was for nothing. She was too terrified to move. Gemma opened her mouth to scream, unable to push down the terror invading her thoughts.

A hand covered her mouth, muffling the sound.

Not a tiger but Clyde! Gemma fought, but a familiar voice whispered in her ear.

"It's me, Gemma. It's Gray." Strong arms turned her to face him, as if seeing him was the only way she could believe.

Relief swooshed through her so violently that she almost collapsed, but between Gray and the tree, her body wasn't allowed to drop. "Gray," she gasped.

"Shh." He leaned in close and whispered so low that she could barely hear him. Right. They had to be completely quiet. Clyde might be close, or one of the tigers even closer.

* * *

Gray had found her. Oh, he'd found her!

Thank You, God.

Shivering, she appeared frail and distraught, but he knew her appearance belied her strength. He pulled her to him and held her in his arms until she stopped trembling. He wished he could chase the fear and grief right out of her, but any hope of that would have to wait until their escape. Still, for the moment, he would rejoice in the small things.

Despite an armed man hunting her and bent on killing her, and despite dangerous tigers free and stalking them in the sanctuary, Gemma had stayed hidden and alive like Gray had asked.

Like he had prayed for.

He wasn't sure how she had managed, and this was not the time to ask. Finding that out could wait. Right now, they needed to get out of here.

A voice called out—loud and angry. "Gemma, you're trapped. You have no escape."

Clenching his jaw, Gray held back the anger and let it burn in his gut. The man had some nerve, trapping her inside the sanctuary with the tigers like this. A woman he'd said was like a daughter to him. Clyde hadn't mentioned Gray's name. Did that mean he hadn't seen Gray's approach? Or just that he hoped they hadn't found each other yet? Either way, Clyde clearly expected

Gemma to be alone and defenseless. Gray could use that. But not yet.

"Come on," Gray whispered. "We're getting out of here while he talks."

He urged Gemma onto his back so they could move faster, surprised she didn't protest.

"Be careful of the tigers, Gray."

Clyde continued, "In case you haven't noticed, the tigers are roaming around outside their habitats, so you can't wait it out. I've taken your dart guns. There's only one way out and I'm standing here at your only exit. So you'll have to go through me. But why are you afraid? You've always been family. I'm not going to hurt you. I'll let you go if you come on out without causing me any more trouble. I never wanted it to come to this, Gemma. You have to believe me. Now come out and let's talk it out."

That settled it for Gray. The man was crazy. Did he even hear himself?

But keep talking, dude, just keep talking. Nothing like a villain's monologue when one needed to escape.

Gemma clung to his back, holding her cane, and Gray kept his weapon out. The last thing he wanted to do was harm one of her tigers, but he would protect Gemma whatever it took. He crept between trees and around buildings, watching for

Raja, the bigger, male tiger who recently lost any trust he'd had in his human caretakers.

Across the path, he spotted the sisters. They'd finished off the meat and settled into the grass, but he suspected their current pose wouldn't last long. They wouldn't be able to pass up the opportunity to explore new and forbidden territory. Gray headed away from the big cats and the sound of Clyde's voice. He wanted to put as much distance as he could between them and Clyde. When they started climbing the fence, they might give themselves away and Clyde would come looking—and possibly shooting.

A growl resounded through the sanctuary, much too close for comfort.

"It's Raja," Gemma whispered in his ear. "He's acted erratically since the night he got out. We need to climb the fence now. If he decides he wants to mess with us, then we're done."

Gray refrained from mentioning he had a weapon. She had to see it. But she was ignoring it, not even bringing up the option of him using it. He didn't want things to end that way either. None of this was Raja's fault. He sidled up to the fence and let Gemma down.

"Gemma!" Clyde called again. This time it sounded like it was coming from a megaphone. "Don't make me come in there to get you. I'll have to kill some of your precious tigers when I do."

Fury filled her eyes. The way she fisted her hands, dropping her cane, Gray sensed she was about to render an explosive retort. He grabbed her arms and held her steady, capturing her gaze.

"Don't give our position away," he said. "We have seconds before Clyde or a tiger finds us." He wasn't sure the tigers were exactly looking, but they were wandering about, exploring, maybe hungry and irritated. Even if they just wanted to play… Not a great scenario for any fragile human that was in their path.

Something stirred in the bushes a few yards away.

Ignoring the surprise in her eyes, Gray grabbed her waist and lifted her high onto the fence. "Grab hold the best you can and climb over."

She could have done that herself, but he wanted to give her a head start.

She glanced at him. Nodded. He read the meaning in her eyes. *I've got this.*

More agile than he would have thought, she moved up and across the height of the fence as if she were a child on the monkey bars. But though she moved quickly, she made too much noise. Grabbing her cane, Gray joined her. He couldn't wait for her to go over first. They were out of time.

Once they dropped to the other side, a tiger jumped onto the fence and then back down.

"Raja!" Gemma almost reached for him but held herself back. "What if Clyde goes in to look for me? What if he kills tigers to force me out of hiding? Gray, I can't let him do that."

"Nor can you give yourself up, Gemma." He gripped her shoulders, fearing that Clyde would soon discover their escape. "I care about these animals too. Remember, I chose a career in protecting wildlife. Don't worry. Clyde isn't going to shoot any tigers. It would damage the goods. He wants them healthy and happy until it's time to sell them."

As disturbing as that sounded, it was the truth and worked to appease her. Together they climbed the outer fence and then descended on the other side until it was safe to drop to the ground.

Gray grabbed her cane and held it. "Now get on. I'm going to hide you and then return for Clyde."

She stared into the woods, where there were no security lights.

"It's dark out there, Gray. So dark."

"I have a flashlight. But we won't use it until we have to."

With her on his back, traveling in darkness over the rough terrain, he had to be careful so he moved much slower than he would have liked. Since Clyde had the sanctuary exits blocked, that meant Gray couldn't access the vehicles near the gate without risking Gemma's life. Despite his need to take Clyde down, Gemma's safety was Gray's priority.

Once he found a place where she could hide and stay relatively warm and dry, then he would go back for Clyde. He was under no illusions that the man would surrender without a fight. Considering they both had weapons, Gray didn't want this to end in a shoot-out with Gemma caught in the middle. She was proactive and determined, and he could imagine her trying to insert herself in the middle to try to talk the two of them down. Gray would hide her away to protect her from herself.

Entering the Wild Rogue Wilderness area that bordered to the sanctuary, Gray thought about Coop. He wished he had called his brother for backup. Cooper would have arrived much faster than anyone from the sheriff's department. But then asking for help would be like admitting he wasn't good enough, after all. Wasn't as strong or as smart as Cooper. Those thoughts sent him right back to his childhood, messing with his confidence.

Bad timing.

And so was the sudden downpour as the mist shifted to something more tangible. Even with her jacket on, Gemma would be too wet and cold. She'd been outside in the wet for ages—she had to be freezing. He'd wanted to make it to the old berm cabin that he remembered being in the area, not terribly far from here, but then he remembered an assassin had blown it up while pursuing Hadley Mason, who later became Cooper's wife.

"How much farther?" she asked.

"Not much."

Coming up on a ridge, Gray shined the flashlight and searched for the other hiding place he'd spotted when hiking the area as he surveyed the sanctuary from a distance. A small fissure in the rocky wall—just large enough to slide into and stay dry and, eventually, get warm.

"This will have to do. You stay here and hide. I'm going back to get Clyde."

"No, wait." Gemma pulled him toward her, inside the fissure cave. "I don't want you to get hurt, Gray."

"I know what I'm doing. This is my job."

"Don't leave me here—I'm cold." She pressed into him, wrapped her arms around him.

He had a job to do, as he'd already said, and tried to ignore her attempts to keep him here. But for another moment, he held her. A cold rainy night like this, and what if Gray got hurt when he returned to the sanctuary and didn't make it back? What if Clyde got the best of him? Then Gemma would have to spend the night out here, maybe even get hypothermia. He had to get her at least a little warmer before he left.

"You didn't have to take me so far from the sanctuary. I know what you're trying to do now." Her cheek pressed against his chest, her voice sounding muffled.

"Protect you, that's what." Warming her up was important, but he knew he was staying there too long, much too long. Unfortunately, he could get used to holding her in his arms like this. "You hold on to the flashlight. Keep it off, as much as possible. I don't want anyone following the light."

Would Clyde still be at the sanctuary? Was he gone by now, on the run? Or was he searching for Gemma, figuring out that Gray was helping her?

At least Gray had saved the girl. And God willing, he would get the bad guy. A twig snapped behind him.

Pain ignited in his head. Darkness edged his vision and then everything went black.

SIXTEEN

Gray stiffened and then his body went limp against her and the flashlight fell away, igniting ghostly shadows.

"Gray?" What—

His weight pulled her down, down, down… His arms fell away.

Hands desperately gripping him, she tried to hold him up. Her pulse roared in her ears. What was happening?

Despite her efforts, he dropped to the ground. Gemma was helpless to stop him, her mind scrambling to comprehend.

A face came into view. The reason for Gray's collapse became clear when she saw the gun in his attacker's hand, held with the butt out. He must have struck Gray on the head. Gemma screamed and pressed deeper into the fissure, the rock wall cutting into her back. Light from Gray's dropped flashlight carved dark-shadowed lines across the face she recognized.

How had he followed them so closely? Found them in this dark, rainy night? Gray had been so careful. But carrying Gemma had slowed him down and distracted them both.

"Clyde?" her voice creaked out, constricted with fear.

He glared at her. "You couldn't just leave well enough alone, could you?"

Gemma wasn't sure what he was talking about, exactly. She didn't want to aggravate him or cause him to hurt Gray again, but she had never been one to idly stand by. And now, her life and Gray's might depend on her ability to protect them. Ignoring the sting of pain threading up her leg, Gemma launched at Clyde, screaming at him. Shrieking for all she was worth. Maybe someone else was out here and would hear her.

"Why are you doing this? Can't you just leave us alone?" *Leave the tigers and go!*

"Me? Why couldn't *you* just leave *me* alone? You've messed up my plans. I tried to steer you in the right direction. But you couldn't just stay the sweet and naive girl I'd always known." Clyde stepped over Gray and into the fissure, forcing her back against the wall. "And now, look what you've done. I'll have to sacrifice you in order to keep my network going. I'm on the verge of a very big deal."

He gripped her arm and squeezed. Pain radiated and Gemma winced as he tugged her out of the small cave and into the light rain. "Get your cane. I'm not going to carry you."

"And I'm not going anywhere with you."

"I'm going to drag you if you won't walk."

Gemma grabbed her cane, but she couldn't keep up with him. "What about Gray? We can't just leave him here." He could need medical attention.

Then she realized her mistake. *Idiot!* Gray would have been better off left behind.

"You're right, I have to make sure he's dead." He chambered a round.

"No!" Gemma threw herself on Gray, covering his body.

Clyde sighed. "You're determined to stand in my way at every turn, aren't you?"

He pulled her off Gray like she was a small sack of groceries. "I can't leave behind a dead federal agent. I made that mistake before with a game warden years ago. Better if he just goes missing along with you."

Gemma glared at him. Something in his face changed, morphed into…what—grief? "Gemma, I… This isn't how I wanted things to turn out."

"And I'm supposed to feel sorry for you?" She wished she had a cane that doubled as a weapon as some others did.

"I need you to help me carry him."

What? "How can I help carry him?"

"Do it, or I swear I'll shoot him now and be done with it."

Gemma slipped under Gray's arm on her right side and steadied herself with her cane on the left. Clyde took his other side. Traveling in the dark through the less than welcoming terrain forced them to move slowly, but Gemma did her best. She didn't want to give Clyde a reason to hurt Gray. Ignoring her own discomfort and her aching, trembling leg, she had no choice but to do as Clyde asked and pray her leg wouldn't give out. And she continued the prayer silently as they hiked.

God, please, help us. Save Gray. Help us out of this mess. And please...

Gemma nearly lost herself in a quiet sob, but she wouldn't give Clyde the satisfaction of seeing her cry.

Please, can you mend my heart? This man whom I loved like a father and thought I could trust has betrayed me in the worst way. Hadn't she known not to trust? And yet she'd thought Clyde was the exception to the rule. She'd known this man, her family had known and trusted him as well. If he would betray her, then whom could she trust?

Come on, Gray, wake up!

A lone figure hiked toward them, his form a

mere shadow in the security lights from the sanctuary. Her heart jumped. Someone to help them? Except Clyde had a gun and would shoot before the person was the wiser.

"Help!" she called out. "Help us, please. But be careful. He's got a gun!"

But the figure continued toward them as though he hadn't heard her.

Clyde didn't scold her for calling out, nor did he lift his pistol to shoot the new arrival or act as though he should run and hide. Her mind finally admitted what her heart didn't want to see—this person was an accomplice, which meant that someone else at Tiger Mountain had betrayed her.

Even if Gray were to wake up now, he couldn't overpower two men. But who was it? Gemma wanted to face the other traitor. As he approached she could just make out a few things. He wore a cap tugged low and his jacket collar hid his face as he took over for Gemma, assisting Clyde in dragging Gray. And then she stood alone, watching the men drag him away toward the sanctuary. What had he told her? She was supposed to wait in the fissure for him to return and if he didn't come back, stay hidden until morning when others were at Tiger Mountain. She was sure Gray would instruct her to run now. To leave him and maybe even get help.

But where could she run in the dark forest?

Without a working cell phone, she couldn't call for help. She would lose Gray forever when the men took him away. She had no idea where they would take him.

"Gemma, you can't hide from me so don't even try. Besides you don't want me to hurt Gray, do you?"

She'd been dreaming, that was all. She couldn't escape Clyde and he knew it. That's why he wasn't worried about her trailing behind them. And despite what he said, she knew he would hurt Gray, regardless. He would hurt them both. In the distance, she noticed a transport truck parked inside the habitat area.

"Oh no… Raja." They were transporting the tiger tonight. With that realization, she stopped.

Clyde seemed to sense she was no longer following. He released Gray to the other man, who dragged him forward and turned to her. "That's right. I've had to move up my timetable. And because you couldn't mind your own business, nobody will be here to oversee the care of the rest of the tigers tomorrow. Your volunteers rely heavily on you to direct them. How long do you think they'll hang around once you're gone?"

Letting her cane fall to the side, Gemma sank to her knees. "Oh, God, please, help us!"

She wasn't sure how long she remained there, but when she looked up Clyde was nowhere to be seen, nor was Gray. The man with the cap walked toward her and then held his hand out as if she would let him assist her to her feet.

"Come on, Gemma. Don't make this more difficult on yourself."

Gemma looked up into Deputy Callahan's eyes.

The flooring beneath him jarred and vibrated, stirring him.

Where am I?

Drums beat inside his skull, which ached so badly that he wasn't sure he cared where he was. He squinted, opening his eyes slowly and saw nothing but darkness. As he lay on a hard floor, the whole structure rattled and shook.

Moving. He was moving. Ignoring his throbbing head, he pushed himself upright, pausing until the nausea passed. What was the last thing that happened? The pain in his head made it challenging to concentrate, but Gray had to try. *Gemma.* He'd been with Gemma, trying to protect her from Clyde. He couldn't remember beyond carrying her through the woods.

Gray wanted to rub his face but realized his arms were secured behind his back. Great. And from what he could tell, he'd been relieved of both his weapons. "God, what happened to Gemma? Please keep her safe," he whispered into the darkness. He'd never felt so alone, so desolate. It was hard to believe God was going to help him.

"I'm right here." A soft voice whispered in response. "You prayed for me?"

Thank You, God. "Of course." He exhaled, feeling the weight of guilt fall away. But they weren't out of this yet, obviously. "What happened, Gemma? Where are we going?"

He heard the scuffle of knees and the creak of the floor and then felt Gemma's soft body draw close to him. He assumed her hands were tied behind her back too.

"Are you okay?" she asked. "I was so worried you would never wake up."

He wouldn't complain about his head. That was the least of his worries. "I'm fine, except I don't know what's going on. What happened tonight? All I remember is trying to get you to safety." Clearly he'd failed miserably.

"It was Clyde. He followed us to the fissure and, while your back was turned, he hit you over the head with his gun. You collapsed and then he almost killed you. Was going to shoot you, but he changed his mind. Instead, he made me drag you. Now we're in the truck with Raja. Clyde made sure to tranquilize him because he is beyond aggravated, but just be aware we're sharing this space with a caged tiger."

His spine stiffened. They had to escape. But

how? "I'm so sorry you're here. That I messed up and now you're in the middle of this."

"Don't blame yourself. I was in the middle of this for years—I just didn't know it. I've been naive for far too long. It's my own fault. I just didn't want to think the worst of the closest thing to family I had left."

What kind of person does that to someone he loved? Family or friend. It was something Gray had never been able to understand, even though he knew it happened all the time. Family members were usually the first suspects when loved ones were abused, robbed, killed or went missing. A sad state of affairs.

But her earlier words wouldn't let him go. He had to know.

"There's something—"

"So why *didn't* he kill me, Gemma?" He'd cut her off. He needed an answer.

"Oh, Gray… I wouldn't let him shoot you. I threw myself over you to protect you and then… then he mentioned he couldn't leave another agent dead in the woods. He'd done it before. Better to have you go missing. I don't remember his exact words. I…"

"You shouldn't have done that, Gemma. I don't want you risking your life for me. Do you hear me?"

"But, Gray…"

Gray hung his head, letting the fury blast through him. "I'm sorry, Gemma. I shouldn't have taken my frustration out on you like that. You saved my life, and I'm grateful. As for his reference to the other agent he'd killed, I was right then. I had a friend and mentor who worked with me when I was a game warden. He came across what he thought was a trafficking ring in this area. I wanted to go with him to try to snag the guy, but Bill got a lead while I was out of town. He was later found dead. And now…now I know that was Clyde. I've been searching for the man heading up this ring, the man responsible for Bill's death. Searching for a way to find him ever since Bill was murdered."

"I'm so sorry to hear that."

"It was years ago, Gemma. But his murder was never solved. Justice was never served. I worked my way up to the federal level so I could cover more ground and find Bill's killer and make up, in a small way, for not being there when he needed me."

"What are you talking about?"

"I should have been there to watch Bill's back. All I could think ever since then was that Bill might be alive today if I had."

Gray had never let go. Never forgotten.

"I think that's the most you've ever said to me about yourself." Her voice was soft in the darkness. "And you think that your friend is the one Clyde killed. The man he was talking about."

"Yes. It's one of the main reasons I hoped to infiltrate near the top of the trafficking ring. Then I received a tip from an informant that sent me to Tiger Mountain."

"Then we need to finish this."

We? "Gemma…" Her name came out breathy. "I wanted to protect you. I tried. And now you're here where you shouldn't be. Things could turn bad and fast, do you understand?"

"Look at us now, Gray. I think they already have. But what can we do with our hands tied?"

"Maybe we can fix that. I keep a small knife in my belt." At least he hoped they hadn't searched him that thoroughly. "I'm going to need your help to get it out."

"Okay."

"Position yourself with your back and your hands toward me and then I'll talk you through it."

Gray maneuvered himself so that Gemma could search for the small knife tucked on the inside of his belt. It was far from easy. Once she had it in her fingers, he turned so she could hand it over to him. He worked it open and cut away his ties and then hers.

She rubbed her wrist. "What are we going to do now?"

The truck downshifted and turned, slowly rolling over a few potholes. "Did you learn anything on the computer or did Clyde say anything about where he had the tigers delivered?"

"Yes. The trucking company was delivering to a warehouse. It didn't have an address so much as directions. Something about Smith's Flat Road, then five miles up County Road 493 and then Forest Road 22."

"Oh, that's just great." He'd definitely need to get ahold of Cooper, who knew this region better than anyone, even the sheriff's department.

"At least we've only been in the truck for a couple of hours, so it isn't that far."

"Maybe he'd been going there instead of Portland, like he told you."

"Could be," Gemma agreed. "But if that's where we're going now, then we should be almost there."

The sound and feel of the driver steering the truck into a warehouse confirmed her words. Someone opened and closed the door of the cab.

"Okay," he whispered. "Time to keep our voices down."

Men talked and laughed. Not good. How many men were here?

The muffled sound of a tiger in distress had Gemma squirming. Gray gripped her arm. "We have to get out of here before they open the truck."

He detected the subtle shake of her head as her hair tickled his cheek. "How can we get out? It's locked from the outside."

Then someone jostled with the lock on the only exit.

Gray's heart pounded. "Let's go."

Quietly they crawled around the tiger's cage to hide behind it, but hiding would only work for so long. Gray prepared himself to take the men down one at a time. He had the advantage of surprise. They weren't expecting him to be untied or armed, even if it was just with a small knife. He hoped he would only have to face one man.

The voices sounded as if most of the men were headed off in another direction. He released the breath he'd held. At least he wouldn't have to face them all at once.

The door of the truck rolled up and stopped a third of the way. It looked like there was only one man standing there.

Someone drew the lone man's attention. He stepped from the truck, leaving the door open, and moved to the side. Gray heard him speaking with another man about an urgent timeline for the delivery of the tiger parts. He cringed. Had Gemma heard too?

He leaned in and spoke quietly into her ear. "Now's our chance." Eyes wide, she shook her head.

He sent her a look. They had no other choice. She gave him a subtle nod.

The light from the warehouse illuminated a good portion of the back of the truck, eliminating Gray's advantage of surprise. One finger to his lips conveyed a silent message. *Keep as quiet as possible.* Then he tugged her hand and gently pulled her out from behind the cage. By the look of it, her permanently injured leg did not want to cooperate, but she made her steps as smooth and silent as she could manage. Hopefully the men would just think the tiger or their captives were stirring. They did not seem concerned and continued their increasingly heated discussion. Gray could use that to his advantage.

They had to be quiet and yet move quickly. At the edge of the trailer, Gray peered out of the small opening the partially raised door afforded them to make sure they could escape without notice. He stealthily hopped down and held his arms out for Gemma. He had to get her somewhere safe and contact his superiors and the authorities to let them know what was going on.

Otherwise, no one would find Gemma or Gray until it was far too late for them or the tigers.

The man who had opened the door suddenly appeared at Gray's side, surprise evident in his features as he lifted his weapon.

SEVENTEEN

Gemma froze, fear cutting off her scream.

Gray slammed his hand into the man's throat and disabled his weapon before the man even had a chance to call out to his friend. He caught the man before he slumped to the ground. This special agent who had infiltrated Tiger Mountain had skills that she should have expected but instead left her surprised. The speed at which he'd acted took her breath away.

She thought back to the many times at the sanctuary he'd acted quickly or handled a situation with confidence, like saving her from the rockslide. She should have suspected then that there was much more to him than a computer programmer who loved wildlife.

Gray's biceps distended and his face turned hard as he lifted the man, pulling her from her thoughts. Assisting him, she helped slide the man up inside the truck.

Then Gray helped her out of the truck. He

tucked the man's weapon into his belt. Searched him quickly and found a radio, then looked at her, studying her. It seemed there was much more in his assessment than merely making sure she wasn't hurt. What was it? Admiration? Whatever it was, her heart warmed.

Stop it! She was too vulnerable when she was near him. But nothing she could do about that now.

He gestured that they were going to make a run for it, a question in his eyes.

Are you ready?

No. Never. She would never be ready for this, but what choice did they have? She nodded.

He gripped her hand and peered around the side of the truck. For the moment, they were alone in the warehouse, except for another tiger in a cage in the far corner. Caesar!

Before she could react, Gray lifted her in his arms. In all that had gone on, she'd lost her cane, but it didn't matter. He crept quickly, closing the distance between the truck and a stack of crates against the wall. In the shadows behind the crates, Gray gently put her on her feet.

"Why didn't you let me ride on your back?" she whispered.

"You'd be too exposed if someone shot at us."

He thought of everything, this guy.

But what did their meager attempt to hide do

for them? "They're going to discover us gone when they come for the tiger."

He nodded his agreement, but he didn't seem to be in a rush. Maybe he thought they had a few minutes until anyone came to check on the guy Gray had fought. Had Gray killed the man with the strike to his throat? Gemma didn't know. She hadn't asked, and she wasn't sure she *wanted* to know.

He grasped her arms and leaned in close to whisper softly. "We need to get out of this warehouse, but I need to contact my superiors. You're sure there wasn't an actual address?"

She nodded. GPS couldn't find that address out here, hence the shoddy directions. Regardless, this was going down tonight. But it seemed to her that Gray was taking too long to decide what they should do next. She could imagine what he might be thinking. Get Gemma to safety or call for help? Even if he could hide her somewhere, they couldn't get far enough away before they were discovered missing. Clyde would find her in these mountains, just like he had earlier that night. "I have an idea," she said.

He held her gaze, waiting.

She pointed at the crates. "I can hide in there. I'll be safe and you don't have to worry about me when you go to call for help."

He frowned and opened his mouth, but she cut

him off. He couldn't keep carrying her around. And she couldn't move fast enough to keep up with him on her own.

"It's the only way."

Finally, he nodded and, together, they found an almost empty crate of wood chips surrounded with other crates that could shield her from sight. Gemma climbed inside. At least it was large enough she could stretch her legs. But she wondered what else the crates held. Tiger body parts? Nausea swirled. She ignored it, willing it to pass.

"This is an old lumber mill, isn't it?" she asked.

"I think you're right. Now that we're out of the truck, I can smell the sawdust, chips and bark. They probably still have the saws..." Gray's voice trailed away.

She understood why he didn't want to finish the sentence. "Hurry, Gray. We have to get out of here."

He nodded his agreement.

Just before he shut her in, he leaned close. "Stay hidden in the crate. No matter what you hear, don't come out."

He was so close that she trembled. Maybe that was her fear of what this night might hold for either of them. Or maybe it was something else. Something she still wasn't ready to admit. His face hovered right at her cheek, and she caught a whiff of his musky scent. Gray pressed his lips softly against hers. Then he backed away. Closed the crate and loosely secured it.

Tonight, they would stop the trafficking insanity, at least, Tiger Mountain's involvement, and possibly the larger trafficking ring would be exposed as well. She had to believe that. Cling to that hope.

To distract herself from the danger she knew she was in, she pressed her finger against her lips where he'd kissed her. Why had he done that? Was he afraid something would happen to him and he just wanted to say goodbye to her—a friend in the war against wildlife trafficking? Or had there been more behind the kiss, just like there was more behind the man? Gemma found herself hoping and praying for the latter but quickly hid it away inside a dark crate in her mind. Hadn't she learned already that she couldn't truly trust anyone? No matter how long or how well she thought she knew them. Not even law enforcement.

Like Deputy Callahan. Yet another person... Oh, no. She'd been about to tell Gray when he'd demanded to know why Clyde had changed his mind about killing him. His questions had led the conversation elsewhere, and Gemma had forgotten. Did Gray already know he couldn't trust Deputy Callahan? Gemma cupped her hand over her mouth to stifle her gasps. She should have tried harder to warn him!

Oh, Gray, be careful.

Though closed up inside the crate, she wasn't completely in the dark. Light spilled through the slats. Through a gap in the boards she noticed a thin space between the crates from which she could observe part of the warehouse. She heard voices. The men were returning. Soon they'd be searching for their missing partner-in-crime.

The rolling door on the truck slid open. Then shouts resounded.

Gray, please get out of here!

With the shouts, Gray knew he'd lost the element of surprise.

Skirting the wall of the lumber mill warehouse, he remained in the shadows. Five men ran into the warehouse, spilling through a side door. Where was Clyde? Had he remained at the warehouse to make sure the tigers, as well as his human captives, were dealt with appropriately? Gray suspected he would question them both to learn what they knew and who they had told before they were disposed of. And there was a good chance that Clyde would be shutting down this arm of his operation until things settled down again. Was that what had happened years ago when Gemma's uncle had died? And then when things were quiet and suspicions had died, he'd seized the opportunity to work with Gemma to build Tiger Mountain?

If Gray took the man into custody, cutting the proverbial head off the snake, then he could likely gain control of the warehouse tonight. But he absolutely could not let the head of the trafficking ring get away.

Where are you, Clyde?

Standing here wouldn't help him find the man. So, for now, he needed to focus on his other priority—calling for backup.

Gray quickly slipped out the door through which the men had entered and searched for an office with a phone or computer or even a two-way radio. With the radio he'd retrieved from the man at the truck, he could possibly monitor the other men's movements but he couldn't call out for help with it. Fluorescent lights flickered and popped in the hallway, one of them going dark. He held his weapon out, ready to use it. With each door he passed, he waited and listened, and then he tried the door.

Finally he found one unlocked and empty. It was full of cleaning supplies. The scent of Pine-Sol accosted him.

At the sound of rushing footsteps, he slipped inside and closed the door, remaining there until the hall was empty again.

Why hadn't the sheriff or a deputy shown up to

prevent Clyde from abducting Gemma and Gray in the first place? Irritation had him grinding his teeth. Even if he made contact and called for help, it might take too long for help to get here if they weren't already on their way. He could only hope that Sheriff Kruse would discover the directions to the warehouse as Gemma had and then maybe recognize the old lumber mill.

Regardless, if Gray had only one chance at a callout, then it had better be good.

He stepped out of the cleaning closet and tried a couple more doors, the last one revealing an office with a desk and filing cabinet.

Yes! At least their disappearance from the truck had summoned everyone to the main room of the warehouse, leaving this office unguarded and giving him the opportunity to find and use a phone. He hoped no one thought to look inside the crates.

God, please keep Gemma safe. Please help us to stop this.

Gray shoved away his worry. He couldn't help Gemma if he didn't stay on task, sharp and focused.

He locked the door behind him and then hurried to the desk, hoping to find a phone.

In this region of the forest, there were no telephone poles hence a landline phone couldn't be installed. And a cell phone would be difficult if it worked at all. But if he were running an operation like this, he would at least have Internet connected via satellite and use VoIP—voice over Internet protocol—for his phone. Though it wasn't optimal, it was better than trying to get a cell signal and a satellite phone needed line-to-sight. In these woods that would be troublesome as well.

And there, on the desk, sat the phone he'd suspected he would find. He called his brother Coop and left a voice message with all the details. He wished he would have gotten his brother in person, but he could count on Coop to find the county road address of the old lumber mill hidden away in the mountains and get Gray all the help he needed here as quickly as he could.

Then Gray called Mark, his superior, and got the man. He communicated what was happening and, as he stirred the desktop computer awake, he realized he had hit the mother lode. The information he saw before him could serve to cripple the trafficking ring if not completely shut it down.

Someone tried the doorknob and found it locked.

Gray set the phone on the desk without disconnecting, so that Mark could hear everything, and grabbed his weapon. Had they heard his conversation?

He stepped away from the computer and hid

behind the filing cabinet. Cursing resounded outside the door. A familiar voice but not Clyde's. Who was it?

He didn't have to wonder too long. The man kicked in the door and stepped inside, holding his weapon out. Gray sagged in relief and stepped out from behind the cabinet, lowering his own weapon.

"I'm so glad you found us." Took them long enough.

Deputy Callahan's sturdy form filled the door.

EIGHTEEN

Dressed in his everyday clothes and wearing a baseball cap, Deputy Callahan kept his weapon pointed at Gray. "Put your gun on the ground and kick it over. Then keep your hands where I can see them and step away from the cabinet."

Gray would never give his brothers in law enforcement any trouble, but... "Wait, what are you doing? I'm a special agent working this case. Trying to stop this trafficking ring. Didn't Kruse tell you? I called for assistance at Tiger Mountain earlier tonight." Wasn't Callahan answering that call for help, following the clues to the warehouse?

"Drop the gun now, Wilde."

Gray did as the man asked, kicking his gun forward but not enough to send it straight into Callahan. The gun stopped about halfway between them. The man glared at him.

"Callahan. What are you doing?"

Whose side was Callahan on anyway? The sinking feeling in Gray's gut told him that he already knew the answer to that. He always went into things suspecting everyone, including law enforcement individuals. And Callahan, in particular, had always rubbed him the wrong way. Still, he'd give the guy the benefit of a doubt. "So we're good, right? Can I have my gun back now?"

Regret surged in the deputy's gaze. "I'm sorry, Wilde."

Clyde stepped into the room behind Callahan. "I went through your things at your rental house and found out who you are. I knew you were up to something."

Glowering at Deputy Callahan for his duplicity, Gray considered his weapon on the floor. Could he make a grab for it? "I guess this means the law isn't coming."

"That's right," Clyde gloated.

"I'm all you're going to get for now," Callahan said.

Gray saw that uncertainty hung in Callahan's gaze. Was he in on this for the profit? Or was he being coerced into helping Clyde with this operation? Gray could guess how things had gone down. He'd seen it all too often. Maybe Callahan had been paid a little to look the other way. Needed the extra money. Didn't think it would harm anyone. But then he was in too deep, and Clyde had him by the throat, able to ruin his reputation or even get him arrested by revealing the bribes he'd taken. And holding that threat over Callahan's head would just force him to fall deeper and deeper into the crimes.

"Where's Gemma?" Clyde asked.

"She's long gone." Gray had to get them apart, distract them somehow so he could go for the gun. "You'll never catch her."

Clyde laughed. Had the man ever cared about her? To Callahan, he said, "Tell the men to keep searching the woods. She couldn't have made it very far."

Callahan nodded and then disappeared through the door.

"You make me sick," Gray said to Clyde. "Don't you care about her? When we first met you told me she was like a daughter to you. You tried to convince me you had her best interest at heart and you didn't want anyone to hurt her. Now look who's hurting her." Gray spat the words, hoping to distract Clyde with his animosity.

"Of course I care about her, but not more than I care about myself. I wouldn't have hurt her if you hadn't forced my hand. Without you sticking your nose in, she would still be safe at the cabin tonight, remaining clueless in her naïveté. Clueless and happy."

He let the anguish he felt at the truth of Clyde's words show. Except, the harassment started before he'd ever shown his face at Tiger Mountain.

Before he said more, he waited until he heard the deputy exit through the door. "Don't kid yourself. She would have learned the truth sooner or later."

"You're the one who stole her life from her, Special Agent Grayson Wilde. And when I'm done with the two of you, you won't have time to even try to forgive yourself before you die."

Gray dove for the gun. A round had already been chambered and he fired at Clyde—who pulled his own weapon—before rolling behind the desk. Gunfire clanked against the metal desk. Gray ducked. He heard scuffling as Clyde tried to exit through the door, but Gray aimed and fired again, trying to stop his retreat. Clyde whirled and shot at Gray.

Gray remained in position and aimed for center mass, shooting a third time, and hitting Clyde in the chest. The man dropped.

He didn't move.

Now, to stop the others. Except Gray heard footfalls in the hallway. Callahan? No, no, no. He didn't want to shoot the man if he didn't have to. He remained hidden behind the desk and waited. Gemma stepped awkwardly into the room, her arm twisted at an angle, and then Callahan completed the image.

"What the—" Callahan started to say before taking the scene in at a glance. He pressed his weapon to Gemma's head. "Come out, or I'll kill her."

He didn't think Callahan wanted to kill Gemma and get himself in even deeper water. But desperation often caused men to do terrible things they wouldn't otherwise do.

Sweat slicked Gray's palms. Clyde's words echoed through his ears, reminding him that if Gemma died tonight, it would be his fault. Just like it was his fault for not being there for Bill.

No. He couldn't let himself think like that. Gemma was still alive right here and right now—and Gray was going to see to it that she stayed that way. This time, Gray knew what to do. He wasn't about to give up his advantage or risk her life. He aimed at Callahan's head, dead center, and fired his weapon. Callahan dropped next to Clyde.

Gemma screamed and fell to her knees. Cupping her hand over her mouth, she sobbed at the horror of what she saw, sorrow in her gaze taking in Clyde's still form.

Gray rushed to her side.

Clyde reached out and grabbed her wrist, eliciting a yelp from her. So he wasn't dead. Yet. He wouldn't survive that shot without serious medical attention. Gray pulled off his jacket and pressed it against the wound in his chest to staunch the flow. He pressed Gemma's hand in place. "Hold it there."

"Clyde," she said through tears. "How could you do this? I trusted you."

Checking Callahan, Gray confirmed what he already knew. The deputy was dead. Gray blew out a breath and stood to his feet, positioning himself in the doorjamb. He watched the door at the end of the hallway in case any other hostiles decided to join the party.

"I feel sorry for you, Gemma," Clyde said. "Sorry you trusted a man like me. You were right that your uncle was murdered. He wanted a bigger percentage of the cut. When the rumors started that the animals were mistreated, the sanctuary came under a lot of scrutiny. Your uncle was afraid of an investigation. And then he got so scared that everything was going to fall apart that he decided he was going to tell you everything. That's why he took you for a drive that night. And that's why I had to sabotage the car. You should have died then too."

"No. You're not saying he was part of it. I don't believe you."

Clyde licked his lips and shook his head. "Doesn't matter what you believe."

"And my parents? You're not going to tell me they were in on the trafficking as well, are you?"

Gray could hardly stand to hear the deep ache that cut through her voice.

"No. And they died because of it. They wanted no part of an extremely lucrative operation even though they were struggling—your father believed the next big donor would show up soon. I knew I had to get them out of the way. With my black market connections, it wasn't so hard to find someone who knew how to sabotage a plane. With your parents out of the way, your uncle and I would be able to do business together. But then he started making demands. And I had to start the rumors and put the pressure on him. You see, there's nothing to tie me to anything on paper. I'm a silent partner via my shell companies."

Another sob escaped Gemma. "So many lives lost and for what?"

Clyde coughed. "I started out smuggling wildlife. It was too easy. One tiger or one rhino here or there brought crazy money. Over time, I realized that I had established a large pipeline in the black market. There was no limit to what I could smuggle through my shell companies. And then I had you, Gemma. I felt I owed you since I took your family from you. And Tiger Mountain could supply me with a tiger here and there, as I needed. And over time, the money would earn back my investment and more. The sanctuary would provide leverage for the movement of other wildlife. A tiger, perhaps, that never made it to Tiger Mountain. But I knew better than to think you'd agree to the operation, so I decided we'd all be happy as long as I kept you in the dark. But then you started questioning things, asking about the night your uncle died. Spending too much time with agent man there."

"You tried to kill me too. Why?"

"You were in the way. I couldn't let you ruin everything I had spent a lifetime building. I tried to scare you away, but you were determined to stay."

"Wait…wait a minute. That was you? The effigies. The vandalism. Releasing the tigers?"

"Some of it. I got the idea from the neighbor. Emil Atkins. His teenage grandson started the vandalism to help his grandfather, hoping you'd get a clue and leave. I just took it to the next level. It was only a matter of time before you would learn the truth if you stayed—" Clyde nodded at Gray then "—just like the agent said. Sooner or later. I'd hoped you would give up, but when I knew you wouldn't leave on your own, I tried to make it look like an accident. But your agent stood in the way. He…protected you."

"What about Wes, Clyde? Why did you kill him?" Gray asked. He wanted to know everything before the answers died with the man.

"I brought him in. He needed money. Sick relative or something. So I paid him on the side. He was the one to leave the effigies, to escalate the trouble. Then he decided he wanted more money or he was going to go to the sheriff."

"So just like when my uncle wanted more, you killed him."

Clyde didn't answer. He let out one last breath and then…nothing more.

Shouts resounded again in the warehouse and boots clomped toward the door. Even with two extra weapons—Clyde and Callahan's—Gray wasn't sure he had enough rounds to hold off half a dozen armed men until help arrived.

He glanced to Gemma. Her wide eyes told him she knew their time had run out.

Gemma gagged on the pungent scent of cleaning supplies that overwhelmed the closet.

"Hurry!" Gray urged her all the way inside. He followed her and shut the door behind them. Her eyes adjusted as light filtered in from under the door.

On the other side of it, men burst through and rushed into the hallway. She sucked in a breath.

They must have been searching the woods and heard the gunfire. They'd returned and would scour the mill until they found them.

This could not end well, especially when they

found Clyde and Deputy Callahan dead in the office down the hall.

Her breaths came too fast. Would her hyperventilating give them away? She held her breath. Gray must have sensed her tension and slid his arms around her, tugging her close. She melted into him, needing his reassurance, anything to stop the trembling. But his nearness did things to her insides, and she desperately wanted to protect herself from him. From everyone.

With Clyde's betrayal, Gemma knew she couldn't trust anyone. Not even this man whom she cared about deeply, in spite of herself.

Still, she couldn't bring herself to move away. There wasn't anywhere for her to go anyway. In mere seconds they could be discovered. Shot and killed.

If these were her last moments… Gemma let herself cling to him, her face pressed against his chest. Felt his heart beating there.

He held her and whispered near her ear. What was that? Was he…was he praying? Gemma's throat constricted.

How many times had she prayed, hoping that God heard her prayers, her cries for help? Did Gray believe that would work? Or was this an act of desperation, knowing they had no other chance to survive this? He couldn't face off with that many men and guns.

Still, Clyde's words came back to her. This man had protected her and been there each time she'd needed him. Had God been there watching over her, after all? Sending Gray to protect her when she hadn't known who the real enemy was?

Well, even if God had sent him, even Gray was praying for help now.

More than anything, she wanted to trust Gray. To have someone to believe in. But look where that had gotten her in the past?

Gemma shoved the thoughts aside. The only thing that mattered right now was that the two of them survived this and escaped Clyde's men.

Voices resounded, and she felt Gray stiffen in surprise.

"Wait here," Gray whispered and then released her.

He opened the door.

And stepped out into the hallway.

NINETEEN

Gray shut the door behind him and hurried toward the door leading to the two dead men. Inside the room five men crowded around the bodies, but Gray only had eyes for one.

"Coop, I'm here."

Then all eyes turned to him.

And weapons.

Relief flooded his brother's features. "I thought I wasn't going to make it in time and then when I saw this I thought…I thought that I was too late. But then I remembered that you can take care of yourself."

Coop grabbed Gray in a bear hug. Patted him on the back, good and hard and brotherly. When Cooper released him, Gray's superior, Mark, stepped forward. "I heard most of this on the phone while en route, though it was spotty. Thanks to your brother, we found our way here."

GPS was especially erroneous in the wilderness and mountain back roads. Mark gave the other men instructions about the crime scene and gathering the evidence from the computers. Gray hoped it would be enough to identify and capture the rest of those involved. But that could still take years.

Coop tugged Gray aside and out of the way. "I won't stay long. This is your case and I don't want to be in the way. But I do want to congratulate you on a job well done. I know how long you've been working on getting this guy who took Bill down. I know how long you've blamed yourself for that, as well."

Gray was speechless. Sure, he could count on his brother, but he always felt like he walked in the man's shadow. He'd never thought he'd do anything to make Cooper actually admire *him*.

"And in case you didn't know, Dad is proud of you too. I know he doesn't say it often enough."

"Yeah, something about wanting to keep me tough." Gray had made his own way, or liked to think he had, and he didn't need his father's approval anymore. At least he would keep telling himself that. But in the meantime... "Wait here."

Gray left Mark, Cooper and the other agents and jogged to the closet. He opened the door and found it empty. "Gemma," he huffed out. He'd left her there in case he was wrong about who he would find, but he'd intended for her to stay put.

Then he looked down the hallway. "Gemma!" he called.

But Gray knew where she'd gone. He headed toward the main part of the mill. Once inside, he spotted her at Caesar's cage. The big cat chuffed, clearly pleased to see Gemma again. That's all that mattered to Gray, as well. Okay, that wasn't true. He strolled her way, giving her some time to process. Maybe she didn't want him to interfere.

For years, nothing else had mattered to him except getting justice for Bill, but he wasn't sure that he'd gotten that today. He'd seen the heartbreak and pain in Gemma's eyes when Clyde had died. The man had used her and her family, killed them. The betrayal had devastated her. And seeing her go through that touched a forbidden place in his heart. He'd ached for her and with her. Gemma had broken through his resolve to never love again.

As he slowly approached, she finally turned from Caesar and Raja, both still alive and well, to look at Gray. A soft smile emerged. Along with it, her eyes held admiration—the approval he thought he didn't need from anyone. He'd lied to himself. He'd always longed to see it come from someone who mattered to him, and there it was in Gemma's eyes.

He stepped forward, closing the distance, and simply gazed into her face, her eyes—they had captivated him from the beginning. A tear leaked out the corner and streamed down her cheek.

"You saved us. You saved Caesar and Raja and…me. Thank you for that."

"You're welcome. I think the credit should go to God."

"I heard your praying in the closet, Gray. I think it's great that you reached out like that and, yeah, I think He answered you."

"He answered your prayers, too, Gemma. Caesar and Raja are safe. This whole thing is over."

She hung her head. He had a feeling he understood her struggle—as glad as she was that she and her tigers were safe, she'd lost Clyde, a family friend. Someone she'd counted on for almost her entire life. This wasn't the time to do this, but he might never get the chance to express himself, what he was feeling.

He cupped her chin and brought her face up. Gray leaned in and gently kissed her soft lips. He had to know if she felt the same way. She drew closer and responded eagerly. Still, was it just heightened emotions and her need for reassurance, or something more?

He had to give this a chance, them a chance. But first, Gemma needed a chance. She needed time and he would give that to her.

Approaching footfalls broke the moment, followed by a loud smack on the back. Mark smiled and shook Gemma's hand by way of introduction.

"This man is one of our best agents. I think you have that management position at headquarters in Virginia wrapped up now, Gray."

Hadn't Gray always wanted that? Some way to prove himself in his competition with Coop for their father's attention? Maybe that was what he'd wanted a few weeks ago, but he'd grown out of that. Didn't need it. Mark said the words, but Gray hadn't taken his eyes from Gemma. He saw in them her disappointment—she knew that with no reason to stay, he would be leaving Tiger Mountain.

And Gray knew he couldn't have both worlds.

One month later, Gemma sat on a rock at Rogue Point, overlooking the Tiger Mountain sanctuary. To her right the Wild Rogue Wilderness region ran up against the sanctuary and to the left were a few neighboring ranches and farms. In the distance, if it were night, she could just make out a few lights coming off Gold Beach.

The last month had been bittersweet. She'd finally learned to trust God. Saw now that He was there working in her life and had been all along. Even when the bad things came by the hands of evil men—free will and all that—God was working things out for her good. And that was the only reason that Gemma could now let go of Tiger Mountain. She had already turned the venture over to new management, new owners, new everything. That was the only way to keep her dream alive—by letting go. The public, donors and government entities would never accept Tiger Mountain as a responsible and authentic sanctuary with everything that had happened. Not with a Rollins in charge.

She let the tears she hated flow freely now, thinking back to the tigers to whom she'd already said her goodbyes. They would have a good home now. And it would be better for everyone that she not be there. It was even better for her, since walking around the sanctuary just upset her now. Sure, she'd built the place, but she didn't like to think of Clyde's investment and the advantage he'd taken of the sanctuary. She couldn't think about that side of things.

And those animals weren't the only thing she'd had to let go of—there was also Gray Wilde.

He'd kissed her, and she'd longed for that. She'd felt the promise of a future there, but it ended like things always ended for Gemma, with better opportunities elsewhere, like that job his boss had mentioned. Even if he weren't promoted, he was a special agent and traveled wherever his job took him.

And any glimmer of hope she'd held in her

heart that he might be the one to stay with her instead of leaving her behind like everyone else had died away at that moment. She'd been a fool to harbor any hope at all, with her history. Gray wasn't too different from the others whom she could never trust—he had lied to her, though she understood why he'd done it. To find the truth and to fight for the innocent.

To bring justice.

It was why she could forgive him.

But why the kiss? It must have been to say goodbye. She'd conjured the hope of a future while he was kissing her goodbye.

That was it.

End of story.

And then… Gray stepped into view on the hilltop, as if she'd conjured him with her thoughts. He climbed all the way up to her. Gemma watched and waited, taking in this new addition to the view—her heart dancing. She'd thought she didn't want to see him again, that it would only lead to more pain. But, oh yes, she *did* want to see him again. She wanted to never stop looking at him.

She couldn't sit and wait anymore and stood, pacing the small flat space, worn by years of people climbing here to look at the incredible view. Gray finally rose to stand next to her.

"Gray."

"Gemma." His smile was tenuous.

"What are you doing here?"

"Don't you know?"

Shaking her head, she looked away—over at the wilderness region. She could just make out a bit of the Rogue River from here. "I don't know. I thought you were moving to the east coast or somewhere."

"Gemma," Gray turned her to face him. "I'm going to take a risk here. Go out on a limb. I don't know if you want me here or not. But I wanted you to know that I'm not taking that job in Virginia."

That news surprised her. She angled her head and studied this man, this beautiful man. Her heart pounded erratically. She feared speaking would give her away. She wanted to say something like *why would I care?* But it would be hurtful and a lie. So she said nothing at all.

"Don't you know by now…?" He began but trailed off.

She sucked in a breath. What was he trying to say? She wished he would just say it.

He pulled her close. Her senses were filled with the scent of him, a cool breeze swirled around them as if cocooning them together. "I love you."

Her heart jumped again. "You do?"

"Yes. And I'm hoping you feel the same way, because I already quit my job."

"You quit your job? For me?"

He nodded. "Do you love me, Gemma?"

Though it was difficult for her to say the words, Gemma couldn't deny the truth. "I love you, Gray Wilde. But why would you quit your job for me?"

"I know trusting has been hard for you. So I took the first step. A leap of faith, hoping you'd believe in me. Give us a chance, more than a chance. And anyway, the job would take me away from you. Too much travel. I'll work on a contract basis as a consultant, but I quit because I want to build something with you, Gemma. I want to make a difference, a lasting difference. We could start another animal refuge, and with my connections we could likely take care of the worst cases."

That all sounded good, but Gray was talking long term. Did he mean it?

"But I'm getting off track here." Gray leaned in and pressed his lips against hers. Gemma thrilled at the love pouring from him, as her senses heightened to every breath, every scent and every sound, and everything that was Gray.

He ended the kiss much too soon for her. "I love you, Gemma. I'm hoping you'll want me around for a long time."

"I've lost so much," she said. "I'm afraid of losing again, but on the other hand I know life is too short to let go of a good thing when I've found it. Thank you for coming back for me, Gray. For giving it all up for me. I'd like for you to stick around for a long time."

He leaned in and brushed his lips against hers. "I don't want to rush you, Gemma, but do you think you could marry me?"

The question took her breath away, but she quickly found it again. Before she could reply, he interrupted.

"It's okay if you need more time. I'm not going anywhere unless you say otherwise."

"Oh, Gray, I've been through so much tragedy. I know that life can end in a moment. I love you and I can't think of anything I'd rather do than become your wife."

* * * * *

Don't miss the first exciting story in the
WILDERNESS, INC. *miniseries*
by Elizabeth Goddard:

TARGETED FOR MURDER

Find more great reads at
www.LoveInspired.com

Dear Reader,

Thank you so much for joining me on this adventure. I hope you enjoyed the story. I set my story in the beautiful region surrounding the Rogue River in southwest Oregon—my old stomping grounds.

As always when researching a story, I learn so much more than I can ever put into the novel. What I learned about wildlife trafficking and how poachers are decimating entire species was disheartening. Whether you're an animal lover or not, God put Adam in the garden to care for the earth—the plants and animals—and God's directive for man hasn't changed.

On a more spiritual note, Gemma has had her share of tragedy and she keeps moving forward in life because she focuses on something bigger than herself. She has a cause and others (the tigers) are counting on her. Still, she struggles in that she doesn't have the sense that God hears her or answers her prayers. In the end she realizes that God was with her all along, working things out for her good.

We live in a fallen world and bad men do bad things, but we know that God is always there working things out for good on our behalf. Don't ever forget that. If you struggle with knowing this, ask Him to open the eyes of your heart.

It's always my hope and prayer that my stories will entertain you and provide a powerful emotional experience, but more importantly that they will bring you closer to the One who holds you.

Once again, thank you for reading *Undercover Protector*. For something extra, if you'd like to see pictures of the Wild Rogue Wilderness region, you can visit my Pinterest board at www. pinterest.com/bethrachg/wild-rogue-wilderness-series/ and look at tigers at www.pinterest.com/bethrachg/wilderness-inc-book-2/.

Be sure to visit my website at www.elizabethgod dard.com to find out about my books and sign up for my newsletter.

Many blessings!
Elizabeth Goddard

LARGER-PRINT BOOKS!

GET 2 FREE
LARGER-PRINT NOVELS
PLUS 2 FREE
MYSTERY GIFTS

Love Inspired®

Larger-print novels are now available...

LILP15

WESTERN (WP) PROMISES

YES! Please send me **The Western Promises Collection** in Larger Print. This collection begins with 3 FREE books and 2 FREE gifts (gifts valued at approx. $14.00 retail) in the first shipment, along with the other first 4 books from the collection! If I do not cancel, I will receive 8 monthly shipments until I have the entire 51-book Western Promises collection. I will receive 2 or 3 FREE books in each shipment and I will pay just $4.99 US/ $5.89 CDN for each of the other four books in each shipment, plus $2.99 for shipping and handling per shipment. *If I decide to keep the entire collection, I'll have paid for only 32 books, because 19 books are FREE! I understand that accepting the 3 free books and gifts places me under no obligation to buy anything. I can always return a shipment and cancel at any time. My free books and gifts are mine to keep no matter what I decide.

272 HCN 3070 472 HCN 3070

Name _____ (PLEASE PRINT) _____

Address _____ Apt. # _____

City _____ State/Prov. _____ Zip/Postal Code _____

Signature (if under 18, a parent or guardian must sign) _____

Mail to the **Reader Service:**

IN U.S.A.: P.O. Box 1867, Buffalo, NY 14240-1867
IN CANADA: P.O. Box 609, Fort Erie, Ontario L2A 5X3

* Terms and prices subject to change without notice. Prices do not include applicable taxes. Sales tax applicable in N.Y. Canadian residents will be charged applicable taxes. This offer is limited to one order per household. All orders subject to approval. Credit or debit balances in a customer's account(s) may be offset by any other outstanding balance owed by or to the customer. Please allow 4 to 6 weeks for delivery. Offer available while quantities last. Offer not available to Quebec residents.

Your Privacy—The Reader Service is committed to protecting your privacy. Our Privacy Policy is available online at www.ReaderService.com or upon request from the Reader Service.

We make a portion of our mailing list available to reputable third parties that offer products we believe may interest you. If you prefer that we not exchange your name with third parties, or if you wish to clarify or modify your communication preferences, please visit us at www.ReaderService.com/consumerschoice or write to us at Reader Service Preference Service, P.O. Box 9062, Buffalo, NY 14240-9062. Include your complete name and address.